UNMOURNED

THE UNMOURNED

(a novella)

By James Baker

Mill Place Publishing

Copyright © 2020 James Baker

All rights reserved. No part of this publication may be reproduced or transmitted in any form or by any means, electronic or mechanical including photocopying, recording or any information storage or retrieval system, without prior permission in writing from the publishers.

The right of James Baker to be identified as the author of this work has been asserted by him in accordance with the Copyright, Designs and Patents Act 1988

This is a work of fiction. Names, characters, businesses, places, events, locations, and incidents are either the products of the author's imagination or are used in a fictitious manner. Any resemblance to actual persons, living or dead, or to actual events, is purely coincidental.

First published in the United Kingdom in 2020 by
Mill Place Publishing

Produced by the Choir Press

ISBN 978-0-9573468-2-6

ONE

Simon stole a glance at his watch: 12.10 pm – so whichever firm had the 12.00 noon slot, they were either running horribly late, or it was just a committal. Not that it mattered either way. He'd fulfilled his own obligations by vacating the chapel on time; and for once he'd even been successful in coaxing his mourners straight across to where the flowers were displayed and where they could now chat freely without disturbing the next service.

It was just a shame the 12.00 noon wasn't there to get the benefit of it.

Normally all it took was for just one person to catch the family as they emerged from the chapel and that would be it: an endless round of meeting and greeting would ensue; the mourners would emerge with the speed of ketchup out of a bottle and all the while the next cortege would be edging ever closer up the drive.

People never tired of remarking that the crematorium was like a conveyor belt, but Simon took constant pains not to reinforce that impression. Indeed, he took a fierce pride in striking that delicate balance between the need for strict punctuality and the need for ensuring that mourners never felt unduly rushed. The objective was to deliver a meaningful farewell within the necessary, but unforgiving confines of a thirty-five-minute slot, and without making the mourners feel like herded sheep.

And what was so bad about a thirty-five-minute funeral anyway? Given twenty-first century levels of busyness and impatience, all that most people wanted was to come and pay their respects, show some support for the family and then get back to their own lives again.

But it was amazing what *could* actually be achieved in thirty-five minutes, without anyone having to go away feeling emotionally cheated or physically rushed. All it needed was for the minister or celebrant to keep the deceased at the centre of a service or ceremony that was concise, but emotionally involving for those present.

On the other hand, if a large attendance was likely, if relatives or friends were wanting to stand up and speak, or worse, if it was known that a would-be raconteur or performance poet was gearing up to treat the funeral as an after-dinner speaking engagement or an open mic tribute slam: well, you needed a double slot for ones like that.

Down by the main gates the glint of dipped headlights heralded the belated 12.00 noon, arriving courtesy of a gleaming Volvo hearse and matching limousine.

The newest and shiniest vehicles were no substitute for the things that really mattered, but Simon couldn't help admiring the cortege as it glided up the drive between the manicured lawns and sentry-like rows of standard roses.

The nearside window of the hearse was dominated by 'MUM' spelt out in white carnations, with pink ribbon edging. At fifty pounds a letter the money would have been better spent on donations in lieu. But right then, that candyfloss-coloured floral confection seemed like the perfect rebuke to the journalist keeping watch from his car. Patrick, the chapel attendant, had made a show of pointing him out when Simon had first arrived.

And more than the journalist, Simon relished the thought

of shamefaced looks from the motley collection of Facebook warriors gathered outside the main gates. Surely even they must have realised there was no sensible prospect of Jonathan Flint's funeral being held at the crematorium closest to his former home.

But this was their chance to grab a walk-on part in the closing scenes of the drama; and they'd doubtless been only too willing to take time out of their taxpayer-funded schedules to be seen doing their bit to prevent Flint from having an undeservedly dignified send-off.

'Okay everyone, angry faces for the cameras please.'

*

Simon gave the donations box a quick shake before putting it down on Beverley's desk. 'Not much in there by the sounds of it.'

His office manager glanced up at him over the top of her glasses. She was wearing the green-framed ones that day. 'Were those protestors still there?'

'Yeah. And a journalist keeping watch from his car. Patrick said he's been hanging around for a few days now.'

'Oh, how stupid! Jonathan Flint won't really be cremated at Gloucester, will he?'

"Course he won't. It's just people stirring themselves up on social media again, that's all.'

Simon pressed two fingers onto a first call form on Beverley's desk and swivelled it round. 'We had another one in then?'

'Yes. Chap's mother-in-law has died in the county infirmary. They're collecting the certificate in the morning and they've got an appointment to register tomorrow afternoon, so I've arranged for them to come in on Thursday.'

'Any idea what they want?'

'All at Lewiston Crem'. There'll only be a dozen or so people there, they think.'

'Good. That's the one's we like.'

The telephone started ringing as Simon hung up his frock coat and returned his top hat to its box. 'Okay, one moment please; I'll put you through,' he heard Beverley say. The phone on his desk started ringing with the staccato tone of a transferred call.

'Colin Armstrong from Collins-Kincaid,' Beverley called out.

Simon sat down and rolled his chair forwards. 'What was the name of the one we've just done for him?' He asked, his fingers poised on his computer mouse.

'Bromley, wasn't it?' came the reply.

Simon ran the cursor down the list of arrangements in progress. Locating the folder for Eleanor Bromley, he clicked it open. 'Yeah, that's the one.' He picked up his phone. 'Hello, Colin.'

'Ah, Simon. Hello. I've received your account for Eleanor Bromley, thank you. There's sufficient funds available at the bank so I'll pass it straight on to them and hopefully they won't take long to settle it.'

'No, they're usually very good. Thank you.'

'You're welcome. However ... that isn't my main reason for calling. I'm administering the affairs of another client who's just died and I'm rather hoping you might be willing to deal with their arrangements too.'

'I'm sure we can,' Simon replied, picking up a biro and pulling his reporter's pad a little closer. He would fill out a proper first call form afterwards.

'I must confess though, Simon, this particular funeral probably isn't one you'd want to take on out of choice.'

Simon's heart skipped a beat. It couldn't be, could it? No, that was a different solicitor entirely. He could still remember the chap's face from the TV. He'd been on it enough times back then. And anyway, there were a couple of daughters, so they'd be dealing with things.

'But you're the only funeral director I would think of approaching,' Armstrong continued. 'The client in question is Jonathan Flint.'

'Oh ... right,' Simon replied sombrely. With thirty-one years in the funeral profession already under his belt, he often wondered what the stand-out funeral of his career would end up being. Gloucestershire was dotted with the country homes of many big names – rock stars, film stars, TV personalities and the like, and he'd always imagined it would be one of them; never one like this.

'I had no idea you were his solicitor. I always thought it was that Hugh Jepson chap.'

'Gosh Simon, you've got a good memory! You're right though, Hugh Jepson was Jonathan Flint's criminal defence solicitor. But Jonathan was a private client of our firm for a number of years prior to his arrest and I used to handle his routine legal affairs. Consequently, I now find myself in the unenviable position of having to act as his executor.'

'Oh ... right ... What sort of arrangements are likely to be required then? I mean ... is there an intention to actually *have* a funeral? Or is it just an unattended cremation that's required?'

'It'll definitely be a cremation. But as you're probably aware, Jonathan has two daughters – both of whom still live reasonably close; and although they've left it to me to make the arrangements, they do still want there to be some kind of service.

'But given the strength of public feeling where Jonathan is

concerned, the coroner is concerned about the safety of the body. So before he's prepared to authorise its release he wants confirmation from me that I have a funeral director and a suitable crematorium lined up.

'I've also had Gloucestershire Police on. They want the funeral to be kept as secret as possible and preferably held somewhere outside of the county; to that end they want to be kept informed so that they can notify the police force for whichever area the funeral *does* end up taking place in.

'So, with all of that in mind, Simon, how would you feel about taking it on for me?'

Images of the journalist and the protesters at Gloucester's Tredworth Crematorium flashed through Simon's mind and he gave a purposely loud sigh.

'I'll be honest, Colin, you've bowled me a bit of a curve ball … But you have always been very good to us, so I think it would be a bit churlish for me to say "no". So I'll say "yes" … I'll do it for you.'

'Thank you, Simon. I'm very grateful, and I know that Jonathan's daughters will be too.'

'Given the circumstances, though,' Simon continued, 'I'd prefer it if we could continue this conversation in person, rather than say too much more on the phone.'

'I think that's very wise. And precisely why I wanted you on board. When would you like to come along?'

'I've got a funeral in the morning, so how about tomorrow afternoon?'

'That would be fine. What sort of time?'

'Um…' Simon swung his chair and reached round for the office diary. 'Could we say two-thirty?'

'Two-thirty it is then. This is having to take priority over my other work anyway.'

'Okay. I won't ask anything more for the moment then. I'll

leave it till we meet tomorrow,' Simon said, feeling like a teenager having a lie-in on Christmas morning. He put the phone down and entered the appointment into the diary. The deceased's surname was normally added in brackets, but he didn't write it in this time.

'Was that about who I think it was?' A visibly shocked Beverley said as Simon swung round again to return the diary to its place between their desks.

'Yes ... Turns out Colin was Flint's family solicitor.'

'Jonathan Flint didn't leave instructions for us to do his funeral, did he?!'

'No, no. It's just that Colin's having to act as executor, and Flint's daughters have asked him to take charge of the funeral arrangements.'

'Do you honestly think we should be taking it on, Simon?'

Beverley rarely addressed him by name, and it was doubly disconcerting to hear her doing so then.

'Probably not. But Colin clearly had his hopes pinned on us doing it. And he does put a fair bit of work our way, so I think it's only right that we should do it for him, given that he's asked us.'

'So there's actually going to be a funeral then, is there? I thought that for someone like Jonathan Flint it would just be an unattended committal.'

'That's what I thought. You heard me say it. But apparently his daughters want there to be a funeral.

'Gloucestershire Police have already been on to Colin though, wanting to be kept informed so they can notify the local police for wherever the funeral ends up taking place. So it sounds like we might be getting some help with ensuring that the funeral is kept under the radar.'

'I really hope you're right, Simon,' Beverley responded.

*

Simon was familiar with just about every detail of the Flint case, but never once had he imagined that it might fall to him to help write the footnote.

It was eleven years since police investigating the rape and murder of a teenager in Surrey made the breakthrough that was needed to bring to an end a spate of similar murders across the south of England. And as the country came to terms with having had a new serial killer at large, the residents of Westoncote, a village between Gloucester and the town of Sherwell, were left reeling from the discovery that the killer was in fact a well-regarded member of their community and a man they'd all been quick to rally round after the tragic death of his wife had left him a widower with two teenage daughters.

Over a five-month period in 2007, Jonathan Flint had abducted, raped and murdered seven young women and girls. He was also prime suspect in the unsolved disappearance of a fifteen-year-old girl from Westoncote.

At the time of the murders, Flint was an established and ironically very reputable motor dealer specialising in sourcing high-end, 'nearly new' cars and 4x4's for a range of loyal clients. While travelling to towns and cities across the south of England buying and selling vehicles, he had identified localities where potential victims could be found – and places where they could then be taken.

He carried out the abductions using vehicles he was due to hand over to clients, then after killing his victims he'd further covered his tracks by stripping the clothing from their bodies, believing this would reduce the possibility of forensic evidence being matched to the vehicles in question.

During interviews with police, Flint said he had forced each of the girls into his car by holding a knife to their chests and telling them: 'Do as I say and you'll live without scars. I'm just going to have sex with you.'

His victims rendered docile with terror, he'd then taken them to secluded locations he'd previously earmarked, where he raped and strangled them.

Flint's first known victim was nineteen year-old Aleksandra Mazurek, a Polish university student working part-time in a city centre bar in Portsmouth. On 13 June 2007 Flint had been in Portsmouth to collect a car from one of his trade contacts. But rather than driving straight back to Gloucestershire, he'd decided to hang around until later that night and cruise a part of the city that he'd previously identified as being popular with young people and students. And when he spotted Mazurek walking along the pavement, he'd felt an overpowering urge to make his murderous urges a reality. 'It felt like fate was presenting an opportunity to me,' he later told police.

He'd pulled over further up the road and got out of his car. Then, pretending to be engrossed with something in the boot, he'd waited for Mazurek to walk past before producing a knife and forcing her into his car. Her naked body was subsequently found in an area of woodland eighteen miles away, hidden in dense undergrowth.

Flint told police that he'd been 'excited by the look in Mazurek's eyes and the way her body had begun convulsing' as he'd strangled her. He said it had made him feel 'incredibly powerful; almost God-like.'

On July 29, Flint abducted fifteen-year-old Lauren Harper as she walked home from school near Salisbury in Wiltshire. After bundling her into his car, Flint bound Lauren's hands with plastic cable ties and gagged her. He took her to an area of woodland where he raped her. He then put his hands round her neck, at which point, according to Flint, Lauren became hysterical and struggled violently against her bindings. But within minutes she too was dead.

On 2 September, Flint encountered twenty-year-old Sharon Patwell in the car park of a golf and country club near Reading, where she worked as a catering assistant. He held a knife to Sharon's throat and told her not to move while he bound her hands and feet. Flint took her to an isolated country lane where he raped and then strangled her, before stripping her body and hiding it in undergrowth.

On 18 September, Flint abducted fourteen-year-old Katie Ritton as she was waiting for a bus in Godalming, Surrey. She was taken at knifepoint, then bound and gagged. In the seclusion of woodland some miles away, Flint raped Katie in the car while he waited for darkness. He then dragged her from the car, raped her again and strangled her. As with his other victims, he stripped her body and hid it with loose foliage.

On 1 October thirteen-year-old Lucy Heaton was abducted from a footpath while walking home from school in a suburb of Cheltenham. Her naked body was found in a ditch behind a layby twenty miles away. A shocked motorist only spotted her body because he'd stepped further behind some trees to urinate.

Later that month, Flint abducted seventeen-year-old Leanne McDonald at knifepoint when he spotted her walking across a car park in Devizes, Wiltshire. Flint said the terrified girl had asked him if he intended to rape or kill her, to which he'd replied that 'If she was good he would only rape her.' On 30 October Leanne's body was found in a field some fifteen miles from where she'd been taken.

On 31 October, seventeen-year-old Ellie Garrett was abducted in Haslemere, Surrey, after she mistook Flint's car for a taxi. Her naked body was found in woodland three miles away, hidden under some fallen tree branches. A post-mortem examination revealed that she too had been raped and strangled.

But Flint fell victim to fate himself when CCTV footage identified a car he'd later sold to a customer as being a vehicle of interest to the police investigation into Ellie Garrett's death.

When police raided the home of the terrified car buyer, they soon discovered that at the time of Garrett's disappearance the vehicle had still been in Flint's possession, awaiting hand-over to its unsuspecting new owner. The car buyer was released, but as the evidence surrounding Ellie Garrett's murder fell into place, the police realised they'd made the breakthrough that was needed to solve a much larger and even more terrible jigsaw of crimes.

The police also strongly suspected Flint of being responsible for the unsolved disappearance of fifteen-year-old Emma Simms in January 2007. Emma lived just a few streets away from Flint in Westoncote and was a pupil at the same school as his daughters, Alexandra and Tara.

The night Emma had disappeared she'd called round to a house where she knew Alexandra Flint was babysitting. When the child's parents returned home earlier than expected, Emma had gone back to Alexandra's house. She left for her own home an hour later, but despite Alexandra later receiving a text message from Emma saying she'd got home safely, Emma was never seen again.

However, when police interviewed Alexandra and her younger sister Tara after their father's arrest, they were both able to confirm that their father had been at home with them and their mother throughout the night that Emma Simms had disappeared.

Describing his motives for his brutal crimes, Flint admitted with chilling frankness that sexual violence was an urge he'd nursed for many years: originally fantasising about it, but later trying to satisfy it with violent pornography.

The first stirrings had occurred during a childhood game of tag with a female playmate. After catching her, Flint had pinned her down and pretended to strangle her. He'd disguised it as horseplay, but it was his first experience of a sexual thrill and from that point on, he said, he became obsessed with any material he could find which contained references to violence towards women.

But as he'd passed from childhood into adulthood, his obsession with sexual violence had been growing steadily more intense until, at the age of forty-two – and with his wife dying of cancer – it had finally reached boiling point.

'Eventually it progressed to looking out for potential victims and imagining where I would take them and what I'd do with them. Then one day something inside me just said, "There's your chance. Go on, do it!" and I found myself actually taking a girl.

'Even when I'd taken her I was thinking that all I had to do was let her go again. But I decided to go through with it and have sex with her. And once I'd done that it left me feeling really pumped and I decided to go all the way, because I knew there was no going back anyway.'

Asked how he'd chosen his victims, Flint had replied coldly: 'I went for ones who were old enough to be sexually attractive, but still young enough to be taken easily. Teenage girls are so careless about their personal safety. They don't pay any attention to what's going on around them.'

But even Flint's callousness had its limits. Asked if he'd ever felt an urge to attack his own daughters, the seemingly horrified reaction had been: 'Never! How could I ever contemplate doing such a thing?! I wouldn't ever do anything to harm my beautiful girls.

'In fact, I didn't realise just how deeply I really loved Alex and Tara until I saw them in the courtroom and realised I might never see them again.'

Flint had been tested a different way: 'But how would you feel towards a man if he'd forcibly taken one of your daughters and then terrorised, raped and killed her?'

'I'd want to rip him apart with my bare hands,' was the reply. To which Flint had then added: 'But my girls were never like the ones that I killed anyway.'

The most extraordinary thing about Flint was not just how matter-of-fact he'd been about his crimes, but also how ordinary his life had been before he'd begun his killing spree. One of two children from a stable family background, he had enjoyed a happy, loving childhood entirely free of the physical, mental and sexual abuse so often a factor in the development of violent sexual instincts.

His adult life was settled, too. The archetypal family man with his wife Helen and their two daughters, no one who knew Flint had even the slightest suspicion about his true character, or that he could be capable of such appalling depravity.

'I was a different man when I was with Helen and the girls. But after Helen died this other thing inside me finally succeeded in taking over my life,' Flint had claimed. But even that statement was disingenuous, because the disappearance of fifteen-year-old Emma Simms occurred before Helen Flint had actually died.

When police interviewed the people who'd known Flint – friends, neighbours and his customers and colleagues from the motor trade – not one of them had a bad word to say about him. They all spoke of a charming, gentlemanly and trustworthy individual, and even after Flint's conviction those same people were still expressing their bewilderment and disbelief that he could have committed such crimes.

Flint's parents were both dead by the time the murders had

started; and his only sibling – his sister Carol, was left so deeply traumatised at learning what her brother had done to his young victims that she'd done everything she could to assist the police investigation, and then completely disavowed him. She even cut herself off from further contact with her young nieces, Alexandra and Tara.

But now Flint himself was gone. All that was left was his body: the last remnant of his physical being. But the task of seeing it to its fiery destruction was going to bring challenges of its own, and Simon felt really quite heroic for having accepted the commission. Like a sheriff answering the plea to rid a frontier town of a notorious outlaw.

TWO

Simon prized the forty minutes of solitude he had each morning before Beverley and Darren, the firm's funeral assistant, arrived for work. He had a little routine, and after switching on the office radio, firing up the computers and settling himself at his desk, he checked the emails. There was something about the nature of email that meant he was always braced for some query, problem or complaint to be waiting in the inbox first thing each morning.

Five new messages appeared: a death notice confirmation from the local newspaper; a draft order of service from a minister; an email from the family with the cover photo for the same order of service; and to Simon's immediate consternation, messages from both Severnside City Council and West Cotswold Borough Council, each carrying the subject heading: 'DEATH OF JONATHAN FLINT'.

His insides twisting with apprehension, Simon clicked on the message from Severnside City Council and was immediately relieved to see that it had been circulated to all the funeral directors who regularly used Tredworth Crematorium in Gloucester.

'Following the death of Mr Jonathan Flint, speculation has been mounting that his funeral might take place at either Tredworth Crematorium or Churston Park Crematorium in Cheltenham. Public emotions have understandably been running high at the prospect of this happening and you will all have seen the gatherings of protesters outside the entrances to both crematoria.

'Although Severnside City Council and West Cotswold Borough Council have not yet received any approach about handling Mr Flint's funeral at their crematoria or cemeteries, out of respect for the murder victims and their families, and in doing what the residents of Gloucestershire would rightfully expect of us, both councils wish to make it clear that they will reject any request for their facilities to be used for the cremation or burial of Mr Flint.

'Likewise, any request for Mr Flint's ashes to be scattered or interred in any cemetery, garden of remembrance or other land belonging to either council will also be rejected.

'Furthermore, in light of the strength of public feeling about Mr Flint's death, Severnside City and West Cotswold Borough Councils also strongly advise funeral directors in the county to reject any request to assist with arranging Mr Flint's funeral and/or the disposal of his body.'

Simon checked that the email from West Cotswold Borough Council was identical and then leant back in his chair, grateful to be alone.

The statement would at least neuter the protests of the rent-a-mobs gathered outside the gates at Tredworth and Churston Park Crems; but it was an unprecedented move by the two councils nevertheless, and a worrying measure of the sheer strength of public feeling in the county.

More worrying still, was the two councils' advice to funeral directors not to get involved with Flint's funeral and Simon began to wonder if perhaps he *had* been a little too hasty in agreeing to take it on.

But he hadn't exactly volunteered. Colin Armstrong had approached *him*.

As a funeral director he could refuse to handle a funeral if the family had an inability to pay for it, and he could refuse to enact specific requests if they were illegal or likely to cause undue offence. But he couldn't turn a funeral away purely on the grounds of what the deceased had done in life. He would have no right to call himself a professional if he did that.

And anyway, what he would be doing for Flint wasn't illegal. Quite the opposite: the dignified and proper disposal of his body was what the law actually required. And neither could it be said that the funeral would cause any unnecessary offence, because it was going to be held in secrecy and in a location chosen with due respect to public feeling anyway.

But what about the victims' families? Would it be an appalling affront to them for Flint to be given a funeral, no matter how plain and low-key? Or would they just assume that everyone had to have a funeral of some kind and that, so long as it was done discreetly, it would simply be a relief to know that Flint was dead and gone?

Nothing could be done to take away the incomprehensible terror and degradation that their daughters had suffered at Flint's hands. But the one thing that could still be done for them was to ensure that no aspect of the funeral arrangements did anything to dishonour their memories.

So the councils' statement didn't really change anything, Simon decided. No matter how secretive and apologetic a disposal Flint's funeral ended up being, someone would still have to undertake it and he was the one that fate had chosen. All he could do was deploy his usual sense of professionalism and try to find some way of delivering the funeral that Flint's daughters were ultimately still entitled to hold for him.

Simon leant his elbows on his desk, clasping his hands and cupping his chin with his thumbs.

Bybrook was a one-horse town, and although he had

acquired a reasonably comfortable living when he'd taken over Arthur Williams & Son Funeral Directors from its second-generation proprietor, the town was only large enough to support one funeral director. Competition, such as it was, came from the three firms in the district town of Sherwell four miles away – just far enough away that Simon had his own distinct patch, but still close enough to keep him honest. Certainly close enough for people to vote with their feet if they decided to take umbrage at Arthur Williams & Son handling Jonathan Flint's funeral.

But would people really desert the firm like that? Once the funeral was over and the dust had settled, probably not. Arthur Williams & Son was a long-established firm and in the crisis of bereavement people invariably went straight for a name they knew. One funeral wouldn't change that, no matter how controversial the deceased was.

And that was assuming that anyone found out about the firm's involvement in the first place. This was the age of the internet and the smartphone and nothing was as safe from prying eyes as it used to be. But with the coroner and the police both wanting the funeral kept firmly under wraps – and whichever crematorium ended up accepting the funeral would doubtless be anxious to do the same – the risk of exposure was as slim as it could ever be.

The more immediate risk was from the families that the firm was currently dealing with. What would *their* reactions be if they found out?

'You mean to tell me that my mother was lying right beside Jonathan Flint?!'

'Was the hearse that you used for my father's funeral the same one that Jonathan Flint went in?'

The current families weren't entitled to be informed, though; and neither was it their place to dictate who else's funeral the firm should be handling alongside that of their loved one. Flint's body would only be a transitory presence on the premises anyway: twenty-four to forty-eight hours at most, and it could quite easily be kept in isolation during that time. The more pressing issue was whether it would be safe to have it on the premises in the first place.

Staying at the funeral home overnight to guard the body wasn't something Simon wanted to contemplate doing. The mortuary was over in the annexe building, so if he camped in the office he'd likely sleep through anything that happened anyway. But even if he sat up all night keeping watch, would he really want to be there on his own if someone intent on doing harm to Flint's body tried breaking in?

The more likely scenario was that he would just arrive for work one morning and find something along the lines of 'BURN IN HELL, MURDERING SCUM' spray-painted across the garage doors.

He heard Beverley and Darren arriving downstairs.

'I was thinking about Jonathan Flint all last night,' Beverley said, once Darren had gathered the information he needed for that day's tasks and disappeared across to the annexe.

'You're not the only one,' Simon replied. 'Have you told Tony that we're going to be doing the funeral?'

'No, not yet. I want to know a bit more about it myself before I say anything to him.'

Surprised that Beverley hadn't even told her husband, Simon felt a stab of guilt as he realised that, in agreeing to handle Jonathan Flint's funeral, he was making unwilling accessories of his staff. 'So what were you thinking about Flint then?' he asked.

'What he did to all those girls and what people's reactions would be if they knew he was going to be here. Especially the families we've already got on the go,' Beverley replied.

'I've just been thinking about that myself. But there shouldn't be any reason for them to find out. It's not as if the funeral's going to be taking place in Gloucestershire. It can't now. Quite apart from the coroner and the police advising against it, Severnside City and West Cotswold Borough Councils have sent out a joint statement saying that they're not prepared to have Flint at either of their crematoria and that they won't allow his body or ashes to be buried in any of their cemeteries either.'

'How on earth did they find out we're doing the funeral?!' Beverley gasped.

'They haven't. They just sent an open email to all the FD's in the county.'

Beverley's shoulders sunk with relief. 'Oh, thank God for that. Can they do that though? Refuse to cremate him?'

'There's no law saying that they *have* to accept him. And given that at least one of the murders happened here in Gloucestershire, it's probably right that they are refusing. You can read the statement for yourself. It's in the main inbox.'

'You still don't think it's too risky for us to be doing the funeral though?' Beverley persisted.

'I do a bit. But someone's got to do it. And given all the work that Colin Armstrong puts our way, I just think we owe it to him to take it on.'

'But it's not Colin's reputation that's going to be at risk, is it? Even if people find out he was Jonathan Flint's solicitor it won't put them off using him, will it?'

'It's completely different for us. Jonathan Flint's body is actually going to *be here* for one thing. And he's going to be taken in our hearse. What if there are TV cameras there to film the funeral? We'll be all over the news.'

'We'll just have to make sure that doesn't happen.'

'How?'

'By keeping it secret. If we can arrange something with a

willing crematorium, we can probably get the job done before anyone even gets to know it's happened.'

'Which crematorium would you use then?'

'I reckon Lewiston would be the most sensible choice. The smaller chapel there would be ideal because it's nicely tucked away. But even the main chapel would be okay at a push. It's not like anyone knows us down there, apart from the staff. And Lewiston's such a random location that I don't think anyone would think of Flint's funeral taking place there.'

Beverley looked back at Simon with an appraising frown. 'You're quite pleased to have been asked to do the funeral, aren't you?'

'Yeah, I am in a strange kind of a way,' Simon replied. 'Whichever way you slice it, it's going to be a little bit of history in its way. But there's only going to be a funeral because Flint's daughters have asked for one, and if anyone's going to be capable of pulling it off discreetly and professionally, then I think I am.'

'Just remember that pride goes before a fall, Simon,' Beverley responded. 'Has there been anything more about it on the news?'

'I'm just going to have a look now.' Simon turned back to his computer and began checking the tabloid newspaper websites first. They'd be the first to get the story if someone did blow the whistle.

'No, nothing new at the moment,' he said with genuine relief, after briefly scanning the various websites.

'You say the email from Gloucester and Cheltenham Crems is in our inbox?' Beverley asked.

'Yeah. There's two. One from Severnside City and one from West Cotswold Borough, but it's the same statement,' Simon replied.

Propping his chin in his thumbs again, he wondered what it was *really* going to be like to do this funeral.

Flint had caused unimaginable horror and suffering to his victims and their families, but his dead body wouldn't be any different to the thousands of others that Simon had handled over the years.

Meeting his two daughters however, *was* going to be a unique experience. What would they be like to deal with? Would they be damaged or dysfunctional individuals? Although would that make any difference anyway? Heaven knew he'd dealt with plenty of other dysfunctional families over the years and always come away from the experience untouched and unscathed.

*

That morning's funeral had been a service and burial at a local church. Hearse direct and no limo; two hymns; no recorded music and a eulogy delivered solely by the vicar, with no one standing up to deliver their own personal tribute. There'd been enough mourners to make it a respectable turn-out, but they'd all been older people and they'd all known what was expected of them for such an occasion.

In other words, a nice traditional, straightforward funeral of the kind that reminded Simon of the profession he'd joined thirty years previously. It was becoming increasingly hard to remember what it used to be like in those far-off, pre-internet times, before the business of arranging funerals had become something more akin to party planning.

Beverley had little to report in the way of phone calls or messages, so with forty-five minutes to spare until he needed to leave again for his appointment with Colin Armstrong, Simon set about the contents of his sandwich box with one hand while typing 'jonathan flint funeral' into Google with the other.

The only new articles were from local newspaper websites reporting on the joint statement from the two councils, and although Simon felt a shiver of guilty apprehension as he read them, they didn't actually have anything new to say.

Instead, he returned to one particularly detailed article about Flint's death and once more immersed himself in the publicly-known facts.

'Two weeks after the opening of an inquest into his death, the body of serial killer Jonathan Flint is still awaiting release to his next of kin. Flint, who was ten years into a life sentence for the rape and murder of seven young women and girls, was moved from High Marston Prison in Worcestershire to Worcester General Hospital on 3 March after complaining of stomach pains, an inquest at West Mercia Coroner's Court heard on Friday.

'Coroner's Officer Anne Morgan said that Flint, 52, was found to have suffered a ruptured abdominal aortic aneurysm which was repaired, but he then suffered a blood clot as a complication of the surgery.'

'Ms Morgan said Flint died on 7 March after his condition deteriorated and that a post-mortem examination subsequently revealed that the serial murderer's immediate cause of death was pulmonary embolism and retro-peritoneal haemorrhage. She then said that the underlying causes of this were deep vein thrombosis and "abdominal aortic aneurysm rupture repair".

'West Mercia coroner Mr Paul Marks declared that because Flint's family had not requested a second post-mortem examination – something they were legally entitled to do – his body could therefore be released.

'But before adjourning the inquest to allow for further investigations to take place, Mr Marks said: "Emotions are understandably running high. Not so much here in

Worcestershire perhaps, but certainly in Gloucestershire and in the other counties where the murders took place. That is only to be expected. And given the public's understandable revulsion at Mr Flint's crimes I fully accept the warnings from Gloucestershire Police that there is the potential for further distress and offence to the victims' families and the local community if Mr Flint's funeral is to be held in the county. Therefore I intend to postpone the release of Mr Flint's body until I have received assurances from his executor that suitable funeral arrangements have been made. I think that is the right and proper thing to demand, given that it would be highly offensive for Mr Flint's funeral to be anything other than a very secretive and low-key event."

'The coroner's remarks were echoed by the parents of some of Flint's victims. Steve Ritton, father of murdered fourteen-year-old Katie Ritton from Godalming, Surrey, said Flint should be buried inside the prison walls just as executed murderers had been until the abolition of capital punishment in 1965.

'Elaine McDonald, mother of seventeen-year-old Leanne McDonald from Devizes, Wiltshire, said any last request from Flint to have his funeral held in his home county of Gloucestershire would be "the final act of a truly sick and twisted man."

'Ryan Patwell, brother of twenty-year-old Sharon Patwell, who was killed in Berkshire, said: "He doesn't deserve to have a proper funeral. He should just be disposed of."'

Simon searched amongst all the other news stories – all of which he'd read before, until he spotted a link to a new article on the website of one of the broadsheet newspapers: 'County refuses to host serial killer's funeral'. Feeling another wave of anxiety, Simon clicked on that one too.

'Following the death of Gloucestershire serial murderer

Jonathan Flint, Severnside City Council in Gloucester and West Cotswold Borough Council in Cheltenham have issued a joint statement saying that they will refuse the use of their crematoria and cemeteries for Flint's funeral. One Severnside City Council official said: "Jonathan Flint has left a terrible mark on the county and we don't want him back, even in death."

'But the manager of a crematorium elsewhere in the UK, speaking on condition of anonymity, said: "I'm surprised that Severnside City and West Cotswold Borough Councils have made this statement, because a crematorium somewhere in the country will still have to cremate Jonathan Flint. There is still a legal obligation to ensure that his remains are disposed of in a dignified manner."

'The unnamed manager went on to say: "If you start picking and choosing which kinds of people you are going to cremate then where does it all end? Refusing a burial can be done for a number of perfectly sensible and justifiable reasons, but if you then deny the option to cremate someone as well, what other option for disposal do you have left?"

'A representative of the funeral industry has also spoken out against the two authorities' advice to local funeral directors to refuse any request to arrange Flint's funeral.

'Mark Portlock, national president of the UK Funeral Directors' Association, said that: "As funeral directors, our role is to care for all deceased persons in a professional and respectful manner, regardless of our own personal views."

'But Mr Portlock did admit that he knew of funeral directors who had received bad publicity and even had vehicle tyres slashed and windows broken simply because they'd conducted the funerals of murderers or convicted sex offenders.

'He went on to say that: "The nature of the crimes for which

Mr Flint was convicted will mean that a normal, traditional funeral can never be held for him. But some kind of arrangements for the dignified disposal of his body will still have to be made. It has always been the view of most, if not all, funeral directors that everyone – regardless of what they might have done in life – deserves some kind of dignity in death."

'But Severnside City and West Cotswold Borough Councils defended their stance last night, with one unnamed official saying: "Jonathan Flint does not deserve any dignity in death. He deserves the same ignominy that he had in life."

'Funeral directors around the county all declined to comment on what they would do if they were asked to organise the funeral, but all of them made it clear they had not yet been approached.

'The body of the serial rapist and murderer, who died in Worcester General Hospital at the age of 52 after being taken ill at high security High Marston Prison, is being kept at an undisclosed location.

'A spokesman for the West Mercia Coroner's Office confirmed on Thursday that until they had received an assurance from Flint's executor that a funeral director and crematorium willing to handle the funeral had been found, Flint's body would not be released.'

After reading the article, Simon scrolled down to the comments section beneath:

> 'Convicted murderers should not enjoy the human rights they denied their victims'
>
> 'Won't make a difference to him anyway, revenge should have happened when he was still alive'
>
> 'They say the mark of a civilised society is that prisoners, however terrible their crimes might be, are still treated with dignity'

'Like Hitler, Stalin, and Saddam Hussein were you mean? Good luck with that ...'

'Put his ashes at the deepest part of the seabed in the middle of the Atlantic – to demonstrate how low a human can sink'

'Absolutely. If some do-gooders want him buried with dignity then bury him at sea and let his bones rot in the cold and the dark along with all the other bottom feeders'

'He has to be buried or cremated somewhere. What do these councils suggest? Do they veto everyone they disapprove of?'

'He was a vile excuse for a human being, but he still has to be dealt with'

'There was no dignity in death for his victims. Why should there be any for him? Take him out and dump him in an unmarked grave somewhere'

'Perhaps on a landfill site?'

'Only problem with that is that under EU rules we have to pay to put rubbish in landfill sites'

'I understand that in the days of capital punishment hanged murderers were buried in unmarked graves in the prison grounds'

'Those were the days ...'

'What other option for disposal do you have left?' I can suggest one: cremate, collect, s**t on, and flush'

'As long as you put the seat back down afterwards'

Simon couldn't help but feel a thrill of anticipation as he left for his appointment with Colin Armstrong. He certainly wasn't without misgivings; but having accepted the leading role in the secret drama that was about to unfold, he was still convinced that experience and a stiff dose of moral courage were ultimately all that would be required.

THREE

The offices of Collins-Kincaid Solicitors were located at one end of a Georgian terrace in Sherwell town centre, where two other law firms also had their offices.

Colin Armstrong led Simon up to a first-floor conference room filled with a dining room-style table and chairs. Like every other room in the building, the ceiling was bordered with ornate plasterwork cornicing and the floorboards creaked ominously beneath the tired grey carpet. The window offered a view of nothing more than the red brick Victorian railway viaduct that ran adjacent to the upper floors of the building.

Armstrong, bespectacled and curly haired where male pattern baldness hadn't yet reached, hunched forward and clasped his hands together over Flint's client file. 'I'm acutely aware of the position I'm putting you in, Simon, and I really am very grateful to you for agreeing to take the funeral on.'

'Well, you've been very good to us over the years Colin, so let's just say I'm returning the favour. But *someone's* going to have to handle the funeral. It won't arrange itself.'

'No ... unfortunately not.' Armstrong smiled ruefully.

Simon opened his folder to reveal the arrangement sheet he'd started for Flint. It was nice not having to stand on ceremony in the way that he would when meeting with a family. 'Can I just check the basic details first?

'Yes, of course.'

'Mr Flint's full name?'

'Jonathan Edward Flint.'

'And he died on the seventh of March at Worcester General Hospital, aged fifty-two years?'

'That's correct.'

'And the two daughters' names?'

'Alexandra, known as Alex; and Tara. But they both go by the surname of Turner now.'

'Will I be having any contact with them, or am I going to be doing everything through you?'

'It's been left to me to make the arrangements, but I really think that Alex and Tara should have some input. This is still their father's funeral after all. And I know that you'll be able to advise and guide them in a sympathetic manner.' Armstrong leant back in his chair and gave a sigh. 'Lord knows they need it at the moment.'

'Hmm,' Simon agreed sombrely. 'Do Alex and Tara have any particular wishes? Or did their father ever express any wishes of his own?'

'Now there hangs a tale.' Armstrong sat forwards again and opened Flint's file. 'I don't suppose burial would ever have been an option for someone of Jonathan's notoriety, but Alex and Tara think he would have wanted to be cremated anyway, like their mother was. But they did ask about having his ashes buried in his parents' grave at Kings Welham in Herefordshire.

'I've made discreet enquiries with the vicar there – the Reverend Julia Forsyth – and she said that she and her churchwardens were worried they might receive a request for that to happen. She said they've already decided that they would have to refuse any request for Jonathan's ashes to be buried in the churchyard.'

'Apparently his parents' headstone has already been

defaced, and Reverend Forsyth is naturally concerned that worse things might ensue if Jonathan's ashes were to be buried there. Not to mention the grave just attracting ghoulish sightseers in general.

'However, Reverend Forsyth is concerned that Alex and Tara might try sneaking the ashes into the grave themselves. Apparently it happened once before, when a family wanted to avoid paying the church fees!'

'Yes, it's not unheard of,' Simon said, thinking of the few occasions when even he had been guilty of suggesting to a family that they go armed with a trowel and quietly slip some ashes into a grave when no one was around.

'Anyway,' Armstrong continued, 'I've explained the position to Alex and Tara, and they accept that scattering their father's ashes somewhere suitably discreet is going to be the only sensible option.'

'But quite understandably they still want there to be some form of funeral service at the crematorium, and I think it would be best if you could speak to them about that. There'll only be three of them going: the two of them and Tara's partner, Carl.'

'I take it you're not intending to be there yourself?' Simon asked. Armstrong rarely attended his clients' funerals.

'No, definitely not. I only go when it's a client that I know particularly well anyway, but I most certainly don't have any desire to be there in this instance.'

'No... I'm sure. And presumably Alex and Tara are aware that Gloucestershire Police are advising that the funeral be held outside the county?'

'Yes, they are.'

'And they haven't got any particular thoughts about where we should try going instead?'

'No, they haven't. It'll be down to you to find somewhere

suitable. I gather that Gloucester and Cheltenham Crematoriums have both said they're not prepared to accept Jonathan anyway. Is that right?'

'Yes. They emailed a joint statement to funeral directors in the county this morning. I printed off a copy for you to see.' Simon took it from his arranging folder and slid it across the desk.

Armstrong pushed his glasses back onto the bridge of his nose and read the email. He looked up again. 'Do you have any suggestions as to where the funeral could be held?'

'My instinctive thought would be Lewiston Crematorium, just over the border in North Avon. We go there quite often. It's just far enough away to be on neutral ground, but also random enough that I don't think anyone would necessarily suspect that the funeral might be held there. Especially if we can keep it under wraps until it's all over anyway.'

'Everyone involved has an investment in keeping the funeral as secret as possible,' Armstrong replied. 'So by all means try Lewiston then, if you think they'll take Jonathan for us.'

'I'll ask them. And failing that I'll just keep spreading the net until I find one that *is* willing.' Simon glanced down at his arranging sheet. 'Do you know what sort of relationship Alex and Tara actually had with their father after he'd been convicted?'

'I don't, to be honest,' Armstrong replied. 'Once Jonathan was convicted, even Hugh Jepson's involvement would have come to an end, so I doubt if even he would know what the relationship became like after that.'

'Alex and Tara must have had their lives turned completely upside down when Jonathan was arrested and I can't imagine how two teenage girls would go about reconciling themselves with knowing that their father had committed the sort of crimes that he had.

'Their mother died a year or so before the murders began, and from what I can gather, the Flints were a perfectly normal and happy family unit until then. But there must have been some kind of latent urge within Jonathan that caused him to go on and do what he did, but whether it was the loss of his wife that finally precipitated it, who knows?

'Anyway, you'll need Alex and Tara's contact details.' Armstrong flicked through Flint's file – the contents of which Simon couldn't help but feel curious about. 'I suggest you speak to Alex in the first instance. She's the easier of the two to deal with.

'If or when you meet them, you'll see that they've both turned out very differently as sisters,' Armstrong added.

*

The two chapels at Tredworth Crematorium were separated by an archway surmounted by a spire. The entrance to the hundred-seat North Chapel was tucked under the archway, while the fifty-seat South Chapel was accessed from the outer side of the building.

The funeral Simon was conducting was in the North Chapel, and as Darren moved the hearse away, Simon remained in the archway, watching the mourners from the previous service returning to their cars.

It never took much for the main car park to fill up, forcing mourners to park along the access roads through the old cemetery and then down the sides of the main drive. But the small area of lawn outside the main gates was restored to emptiness once more now that the protesters had gone.

According to Patrick, the chapel attendant, they'd already started looking bored and self-conscious. But just as the futility of their presence had surely begun to dawn on them, the statement from the two councils had arrived like manna from heaven.

Simon had seen for himself on the Gloucestershire news website how the protesters had revelled in their vindication, before agreeing to disband in a hail of self-congratulation and doubtless no small amount of relief.

Simon turned to where Patrick was busy rolling a cigarette in the shelter of the corner between the chapel entrance and the door to the ministers' vestry.

'What's new then?'

'Roger Stafford upset a family with a service sheet the other day.'

Simon rolled his eyes. 'How'd he manage that?'

'They 'ad a big funeral up here – retired English professor or summat – and you'd think for one like that Roger would make a special effort with the service sheets. But no, 'e just turned up with 'is usual cheap-looking ones.

'Anyway, the family wanted a quotation put on the back cover: "The pen is mightier than the sword". But Roger don't ever check the sheets properly before they're printed and 'e didn't spot that on all the sheets it said: "The *penis* mightier than the sword".'

'Oh for fuck's sake ...' Simon grimaced. 'How d'you go about apologising for something like that?'

'You tell me!' Patrick giggled wheezily.

He lit his roll-up and took a drag. 'So who's goin' to end up doing old Jonny Flint's funeral then?'

'Has anyone been approached yet, d'you know?' Simon parried back.

'No one's said anything. But they'll all turn it down. No FD in the county's gonna want to be seen doin' that sick fucker's funeral, are they?'

'No, of course not,' Simon responded.

With Flint's home village of Westoncote being located mid-way between Sherwell and Gloucester, funerals there had always been evenly divided between firms in both places, and Simon did the occasional funeral there himself.

But Flint had been in prison in Worcestershire for ten years, and for anyone other than Simon there would be no real way of knowing who might end up handling the funeral. His hopes were firmly pinned on it staying that way.

'Nick from Walkers was up 'ere yesterday and they 'ad a family that were due to make arrangements phoning up and asking if Walkers were doing Flint's funeral. The family said they'd go to another firm if they were, because they didn't want their mother lying in the same chapel of rest as Flint.'

'No, I can understand that,' Simon said pensively, fighting down his rising anxiety. 'Was the office here getting many enquiries here before the councils issued their statement?'

'Yeah, loads. They've 'ad all the national newspapers phoning. But Jonny Flint wouldn't ever 'ave come 'ere anyway. This'd be the last place they'd 'ave his funeral,' Patrick said, his eyes narrowing as he took another drag on his cigarette.

Simon gave a thoughtful frown. 'Say for a minute that Jonathan Flint didn't have any connection to Gloucestershire and that he came from, oh I don't know, say Hertfordshire; and that all the murders were committed there. If he was brought here to be cremated, how d'you think it would be handled?'

'We'd make sure it were done early in the morning, before any other funerals took place. Either that or late in the afternoon when everyone's gone. An' it would be kept absolutely secret too. It's so open-plan 'ere that even if a reporter or a photographer was outside the gates they'd still be able to see what was going on up 'ere and photograph it with a zoom lens.'

'And if it *was* done in secret,' Simon continued, 'and early in the morning like you said, d'you think Flint's relatives would be allowed to have a little service if they wanted one?'

'We wouldn't really be able to say 'no' if the cremation was being done 'ere. But we'd keep the chapel doors locked and we'd notify the police that it was taking place, just in case summat did kick off.'

'Yeah, that's true ... Are you still getting reporters loitering around?'

'We 'ad one drive up first thing this morning and look at the chapel list before driving off again. I dunno what she thought she was going to find though. Even if Jonny Flint was being done 'ere we'd 'ardly put it up on the chapel list would we?'

'Course not.'

'I reckon they'll just get whichever funeral director does the council funerals up where the prison is to do it. Just 'ave an early morning committal and get rid of the evil fucker.'

'That's what I think they'll do. If they haven't done it already.' Simon cocked his head towards the open vestry door. There was a loudspeaker in there and Patrick had left the volume turned up so they could hear the service. 'That's the second hymn.'

'Better get back in then,' Patrick said, snatching a last drag on his roll-up before stubbing it into the cigarette bin by the chapel entrance.

*

Simon took his leave of the family and headed across to where the newest recruit to his team of casually employed driver-bearers was waiting patiently by the hearse. With the deceased's son and three grandsons wanting to carry the coffin themselves, it had been the ideal chance to try out David's driving without the distraction of the other bearers being with them. Not that the driving aspect of the job was ever likely to be much of an issue with David anyway.

'Did you spend the whole of your time in the police on Traffic?' Simon asked once they'd got out of the crematorium grounds and back onto the ring road.

'One way and another, yes. After I'd done my two years on the beat I put straight in for Traffic and did that for fourteen years. Then towards the end of that period I was on armed response, and I spent my last few years as a driving instructor.'

'What sort of things did you teach as an instructor?'

'Everything from the basic car course for new recruits, through to the advanced driving course for officers heading for traffic duties. And then various specialist courses like tactical pursuit, close protection driving for VIP's, prisoner escort, that sort of thing.'

'So if you were transporting someone who needed close protection, what sort of techniques would you use?'

'The first thing is to establish what type of journey it is. Regular journeys always carry the greatest risk because they're a known quantity and a would-be attacker could very easily familiarise themselves with the route and the timings.

'It's the same with special events, because the VIP's attendance will often be publicised in advance. So the safest journeys are always the unscheduled ones, because it's much harder for someone to plan an attack then.

'But either way, we always used pre-planned routes and kept to A roads and motorways wherever possible, because all the time we were moving we were reducing the opportunity for attack. And there's also more space for evasive manoeuvres on primary roads.'

'And what if you had come under attack?'

'The overriding objective is always to get the VIP away from danger, so if there's a bit of space on a wide road, you aim for that and put your foot down. Or turn off and use an alternative route if there's one available.'

'But what if the road's completely blocked by the attackers and there isn't anywhere to turn off either?'

'Then you either go for a rapid three-point turn and hoof it away in the opposite direction; or if it's a confined space like an urban street then you'd execute a high speed reverse and aim for a suitable gap – the junction with a side road ideally, but a driveway or even just the space between two parked cars if that's all there is; then hit the brakes and flick the steering wheel as you reach your gap, and let the weight of the engine throw the front end of the vehicle through one-eighty degrees and into the direction of escape.

'It's not the sort of thing you'd want to try doing in this nice posh hearse.'

'No ... absolutely!' Simon chuckled. 'Well, I hope not anyway ...'

*

Unbeknown to his wife, Simon had an ashes interment booked the evening she told him their marriage was over. There hadn't been any unfaithfulness or plate-throwing dramas – he and his wife had simply grown apart. But barely an hour after that fateful conversation, Simon had found himself back on duty in a churchyard.

As the vicar had recited the prayers, Simon had stood with his head bowed, contemplating the little wooden casket sitting in a neatly dug hole at his feet and acutely aware that like the newly-widowed woman stood alongside him, he too was suddenly facing a lonelier and radically altered future.

Six years on, returning home to an empty house was still a glum experience at times, but Simon had adjusted to solitary living.

The only decent thing on telly that night was a police

drama, and as he sat half-watching it, he reflected on his conversations with Patrick and David.

Trying to keep Flint's funeral arrangements a secret would be enough of a challenge as it was, but what if word *did* get out? A £125,000 hearse was the very last kind of vehicle to be putting in harm's way if there was the possibility of a vengeful crowd gathering outside the gates to the crematorium.

And yet, if secrecy could be maintained, then who would take any notice of a hearse and coffin arriving at a crematorium? Flint could be hidden entirely in plain sight.

Simon dislodged the cat from his lap – incurring considerable feline displeasure in doing so – and got to his feet. Amongst the contents of his well-stocked bookshelves he knew exactly which two books he wanted.

Ever since he'd seen the war film *The Man Who Never Was* he'd been fascinated by the true story of how a dead body had been used in a British deception operation during the Second World War to disguise the 1943 Allied invasion of Sicily.

The unclaimed dead body of a civilian had been floated ashore on the Spanish coast after being made to look like a British army officer killed in an air crash while carrying vital secret documents.

It was known that the Germans maintained a highly efficient espionage network in Spain, and the plan hinged around them getting their hands on the dead man's papers when his body was discovered.

The Allies intended to invade Sicily, so carefully faked invasion plans were planted on the body of the dead 'officer' in the hope of convincing the Germans that it was actually Greece and Sardinia that were going to be invaded. It was hoped that if the Germans swallowed the bait, they would transfer the troops needed for the defence of Sicily and the task of the invading Allied forces would then be made easier.

British military intelligence approached the Coroner for the northern district of London for help in obtaining a body that was medically suitable and without any relatives who might claim it for burial. It was then dressed in the uniform of a fictional army major, complete with personal effects and identity papers. Faked invasion plans were put in a briefcase discreetly chained to the body, just as a genuine military courier would have had, and it was then packed in dry ice and transported to Spanish waters in a British submarine.

The body was released into the sea close to the port of Huelva on 30 April 1943 and was discovered the following morning by a Spanish fisherman.

After routine investigations by Spanish authorities, the dead 'officer' was buried in Huelva with full military honours and the accompanying documentation was returned to British consular authorities. But not before German Intelligence had examined the documents for themselves and fallen for the ruse.

German troop reinforcements were shifted to Greece and Sardinia and Sicily was subsequently liberated more quickly than anticipated and with lower than predicted Allied losses.

As Simon flicked through his copies of the officially censored 1953 book and its altogether more detailed 2010 counterpart, he couldn't help but imagine how simple his own mission would become if he could conspire with a willing crematorium to have Flint received under a false name. It wasn't exactly a matter of national security, but it would undoubtedly be in the public interest for Flint to be disposed of as discreetly as possible.

The funeral ceremony would still need to be carried out early in the morning or late in the afternoon just as a matter of principal; but even if anyone did happen to be around at the time, there would be little risk of them recognising Alex and

Tara, because their photos had never been published and no one knew what their new identities were.

As Simon's excitement at the idea grew, he even imagined how it might be reported on the Six O'Clock News: 'And in other news, the funeral of serial killer Jonathan Flint has taken place. Flint is said to have been cremated at an undisclosed crematorium, following a short service attended only by his two daughters.'

Could it really be made to be that simple?

FOUR

'Hello?' A young woman's voice: sharp-sounding and suspicious, but well-spoken.

'Hello, is that Alex Turner?' Simon asked, anxious to get past this awkward necessity.

'Who wants to know?'

Simon loathed that phrase, although for once he was speaking to someone genuinely entitled to use it.

Even after thirty years in the funeral profession he still had to guard against pre-judging new clients during that awkward first call. Bereavement could make people act irrationally at the best of times, but if they were naturally shy and reticent, or rude and demanding characters to begin with, it often served to turn up the volume of their idiosyncrasies.

Most people just wanted help and guidance, but there were always a few who lost no time in making it clear that they regarded having to arrange a funeral as a distasteful imposition and one that came at outrageous expense.

Either way, Simon's responsibility was to parachute in to each client's situation, patiently address their bewilderment, identify and pirouette round even the tiniest individual sensitivities, and then hope to create something meaningful from it all before finding a tactful way to render his bill and exit stage left.

That wasn't to say that his work as a funeral director didn't still require a very particular grace and exceptional powers of empathy, but Simon had learnt long ago that while the vast majority of people were genuinely grateful for his help, no one ever approached him by choice and they rarely wanted to engage with his offering any more than was necessary. They wanted help getting the arrangements made, and in the meantime have the body taken care of, usually in the expectation that it would cost them an arm and a leg for the privilege.

'My name is Simon Thorley. I'm from Arthur Williams & Son Funeral Directors, in Bybrook, near Sherwell. Colin Armstrong of Collins-Kincaid Solicitors has approached me about handling your father's funeral arrangements and he's asked me to make contact with you.'

'Oh . . . right . . . yes. Colin said you'd be calling. You want to talk to me and my sister about the funeral, don't you?'

'Yes. I think it would be very helpful if the three of us could get together and have a chat about things.'

'There'd be four of us. My sister will want her partner Carl there.'

'Sure.'

'But did you say you're in Bybrook? Would we have to come all the way over there?'

'No, not necessarily. Colin explained that you're in Cheltenham and that your sister's over in Ross-on-Wye, so given the circumstances I'd be perfectly happy to come to one of your homes.'

'I'm at work all week though.'

'Well, it's Thursday now, so I was wondering if we could meet at the weekend? Or an evening if that's easier.'

Simon normally drew a line at seeing families in the evenings or at weekends. The out of hours rota for manning the telephone and performing body removals was enough of an intrusion as it was. But this funeral more than warranted giving up some spare time. In fact, it was preferable to shoehorning it into a normal working day, particularly as he was intending to dress in civvies for extra discretion anyway.

'Saturday morning would probably be okay. I just want to get this sorted. You'll have to come to my flat in Cheltenham though. My sister lives at the equestrian centre where she works and the people there will be asking too many questions if they see someone turning up in a suit.'

'I understand,' Simon replied, picturing himself turning up at a riding school in a black suit and carrying a briefcase. 'I'll come to Cheltenham then. But rest assured, I was intending to be a lot more discreet that just turning up in a black suit.'

'That would be good. I don't really want *my* neighbours asking questions either.'

'No, I'm sure,' Simon said, wondering whether Alex or Tara's respective neighbours actually knew who they were. He was intrigued himself to see what they'd be like, because there'd never been any pictures of them in the media or on the internet. 'How would eleven o'clock sound?'

'I'll need to check with my sister, but that should be okay. Do you know what my address is?'

'Colin gave me twenty-four Portman Court, Prestbury Heights, Cheltenham?' Simon replied, subtly altering his tone to demonstrate that he knew how sensitive that information was.

'Yes, that's right.'

'Okay. Well, all being well, I'll see you all at eleven o'clock on Saturday.'

'Can you just tell me one thing while you're on?'

'Sure.'

'When d'you think the funeral will be?'

'That's one of the things we need to talk about. But subject to finding a suitable crematorium and getting all the necessary paperwork up together, I'd like to think the funeral could take place within the next two weeks.'

'Two weeks? I didn't think it was going to take that long! Me and my sister want it over with. We need to get on with our lives.'

'I appreciate that and rest assured I shall do everything I can to make sure the funeral takes place as soon as possible. But there are various things that I'll need to get organised; and despite the circumstances, I do still want to make sure that the funeral ends up being what you and your sister would want it to be.'

'Will we end up with the police guarding it and all that sort of thing?'

Simon had been wondering the exact the same thing, and he was glad that Alex did at least seem to have grasped that the arrangements might well be dictated by security considerations. 'I hope not. If we can arrange things the way I want to, I'm hoping we'll be able to hold a quiet little service and slip away again without anyone being any the wiser.'

*

'Coroner's Office. Terry Gregory speaking.'

'Hello, Mr Gregory. My name is Simon Thorley. I'm from Arthur Williams Funeral Directors in Gloucestershire.'

'Hello there,' came the wary-sounding reply.

'I've been instructed by the solicitor acting for the late Mr Jonathan Flint, so I'm just phoning to make myself known to you.'

'Jonathan Flint ... I wondered what was happening with him. Okay, bear with me a minute while I get the details up on the computer.'

Gregory's tone had already changed from wariness to the more usual air of disinterest so characteristic of all the coroner's officers Simon had ever dealt with; the kind of tone that might be expected from an ex-detective.

Originally performed by serving police officers, the role of coroner's officer had long since become a civilian appointment, but preference was still weighted towards ex-detectives; their familiarity with investigative processes and their experience of precisely the kind of deaths that needed reporting to the coroner all making it an obvious progression.

'Can you just give me the solicitor's name?' Gregory asked.

'Colin Armstrong – from Collins-Kincaid Solicitors in Sherwell, Gloucestershire.'

'Okay ... Has Mr Armstrong explained to you that before the coroner will release the body he wants confirmation from Mr Armstrong that a crematorium has been booked?'

'Yes, he has. I've only just been instructed by him myself, but I've arranged to speak with Mr Flint's daughters to see whether they have any particular wishes before I—'

'You'll need to be very careful about giving in to any wishes from the family,' Gregory put in sternly. 'Gloucestershire Police have already advised them to have the cremation done in secret outside the county.'

'Yes, Colin Armstrong explained all of that to me. There's no way the funeral will be held in Gloucestershire,' Simon replied, feeling unjustly chastened, 'and Mr Flint's daughters know that. It's only the finer details of the service itself that I need to speak—'

'There's going to be a *service*?' Gregory interrupted again.

'Only in the sense that the daughters just want to be present at the crematorium,' Simon said patiently, fighting down his irritation. 'There's no intention of it being anything other than just a few words of committal before the curtains close.'

'Make sure it is then – for everyone's sake, including yours. Although, to be honest, I'd be surprised if any crematorium will even let you do that.'

'Given the circumstances it wouldn't be much of a loss to me if they didn't. But whatever happens, I shall be doing everything in my power to keep everything as low-key as possible,' Simon responded. He didn't need lectures from a coroner's officer about how to do his job – even in a situation like this. 'But in the meantime I thought I'd better just make myself known to you and confirm that it will definitely be a cremation.'

'I don't think there was ever any question over that. The coroner wouldn't release the body otherwise. What was your name again?'

'Simon Thorley. And the company name is Arthur Williams Funeral Directors.'

'And your email address and telephone number?'

Simon recited them.

'Okay, I've put all your details onto the system, and once we get confirmation from Mr Armstrong that a date and time has been booked with a crematorium, we'll release the body.'

'Thank you. Doubtless we'll speak again in due course then.'

Still nettling from having his professionalism questioned, Simon realised he hadn't thought to ask where Flint's body was actually being kept. He'd find out soon enough of course, but he couldn't resist clicking on Google and typing 'west mercia coroner + mortuary'.

The search revealed that the West Mercia Coroner's Office had not long moved into a purpose-built complex that brought the inquest courtroom, administration offices and mortuary together under one roof – and an image search revealed an impressive, modern building.

Then on a whim Simon returned to the Google home page and typed 'murderer's funeral' into the search box. Although nothing of any interest came up at first, he used the titles of the articles that did appear to expand his search and discovered a news article from 2013, detailing how three different countries had all refused burial to Nazi war criminal Erich Priebke.

Extradited to Italy in 1995, to face trial for his part in a 1944 massacre of Italian civilians, Priebke had been sentenced to life imprisonment and due to his advanced age had served his sentence under house arrest in Rome.

But when he'd died there in 2013, Vatican officials had banned any Catholic church in the city from holding a funeral for him and the city's mayor refused permission for his body to be buried there.

Argentina refused to have Priebke back for burial alongside his wife and even his home town in Germany refused to have his body for fear of his final resting place becoming a shrine for neo-Nazi sympathisers.

The ultra-right-wing Catholic Society of St Pius X subsequently offered to perform a funeral ceremony for Priebke at its chapel in Albano Laziale, outside Rome. But protesters had kicked and spat at the hearse carrying Priebke's coffin until the police had intervened by seizing the coffin and whisking it away to a military airport for safekeeping.

Priebke's body was later buried in a secret location.

Alarmed by the photographs of furious protesters being held back from the hearse by riot police, Simon scrolled down to the comments section, hoping there might instead be something to be gleaned from the wisdom of crowds. To his amazement he found it almost immediately, in the form of a comment from a former British military chaplain:

'I once had to take a service for a former concentration camp guard. I couldn't say anything to honour him of course, but I still had sympathy for his family. This all happened after the war had ended and his family had only just discovered about this man's past. But my concern for them did not mean that I was excusing him.'

On reading that, Simon suddenly felt as if a great weight had been lifted from his shoulders. Just like the military chaplain, he wasn't actually required to reconcile himself with the act of arranging Flint's funeral at all. His responsibility was simply to ensure that Alex and Tara were given the chance to grieve for their father, just as any other man's daughters would be.

*

Darren was busy furnishing a coffin when Simon went across to the annexe building.

'Who's that one for?'

'Jacobson.'

'She wasn't that big was she? What's that, a six foot twenty?'

'We're running low on five nines, so as she's a straight to the crem' and they aren't viewing I thought she might as well have some extra leg room.'

'You'd better do me a list of what coffins we've got left then and I'll put a stock order in,' Simon replied, watching as Darren fixed three brass-effect, plastic 'Yorkrem' handles into place down one side of the upturned coffin.

When he'd taken ownership of Arthur Williams, the first thing Simon had done was start using Yorkrems on all his coffins. They looked far more elegant and substantial than the 'Fleur' handles his predecessor had used.

But as he looked at the remaining stock of plain oak veneered coffins standing in two rows against the workshop wall, he knew there was a risk that one of them might soon become the most photographed coffin in the country; and that people might then question why someone like Flint had been sent off in a nice-looking coffin with shiny brass handles.

'What d'you think's going to happen with Jonathan Flint then?' Darren asked, as if reading Simon's thoughts.

Simon tensed. 'How d'you mean?'

'Well, is he still in a mortuary somewhere; or d'you think he's already been secretly cremated?'

'I'm sure it would've been mentioned on the news if his funeral had taken place. He's probably still in a mortuary somewhere.'

'So there's still a chance we might get him then?' Darren replied, just as the phone extension started ringing. Simon ignored it; Beverley was over in the office and sure enough the phone fell silent again after two rings.

Simon smiled and gave a dismissive snort, hoping there was nothing in his demeanour to give him away. Darren was rather an intense young man at the best of times and Simon couldn't tell if he was just curious or whether Beverley had tipped him off. 'I very much doubt it. And now that Gloucester and Cheltenham Crems have said they'll refuse to have him, it'll have to be done somewhere outside the county anyway.'

The phone extension rang again, this time with the tone of an internal call. 'Joanne Barrett, for you,' Beverley said portentously, when Simon answered.

Joanne was the Sherwell local reporter for the Gloucestershire Standard, the county's evening paper. She had been the reporter on duty one Sunday afternoon twenty-nine years previously when Simon had attended his first murder scene, and she had gone on to become a familiar caller in later years, through her reporting of notable deaths and funerals.

The workshop phone was a portable one, so Simon moved back across to the door ready to duck out of earshot if this turned out to be the call he was fearing. 'Okay, put her on.'

Simon waited a couple of seconds for Beverley to transfer the call. 'Hello, Joanne.'

'Hi, Simon. I just wanted to make an enquiry about something, if I may.'

'Fire away ...'

'Have you been approached about handling Jonathan Flint's funeral?'

Simon felt his stomach lurch. 'No ... we haven't. And I'm hoping it stays that way, to be honest,' he replied, adding a slight inflection for good measure. He couldn't lie to save his life, but he could feign ignorance with the best of them.

Seeing that Darren was preparing to staple the 'Cremfilm' plastic lining into the coffin he was working on, Simon stepped outside and pulled the door to behind him.

'You wouldn't be willing to do it then?'

'I don't think any funeral director in the county would, to be honest.'

'Do funeral directors often turn controversial funerals away?'

Knowing that anything he said might be taken down and quoted in newsprint against him, Simon took care with his reply: 'It's extremely rare for a funeral to be that controversial to begin with. And when it is, it's usually because someone has committed a particularly nasty crime – a sex offender; or a drink driver who's killed someone, maybe.

'But because Jonathan Flint's crimes were *so* serious and exceptional and because at least one of the murders was committed within Gloucestershire, I think any funeral director in the county would be reluctant to be involved with his funeral.'

'Sure. I understand. So is the coroner still holding Flint's body at the moment then?'

'I assume so. I haven't seen or heard anything about the funeral taking place yet.'

'So no one can start making funeral arrangements until his body is released then?'

'No, even when a death's reported to the coroner a family can still start making funeral arrangements, but they wouldn't actually be able to set a date for the funeral until they know when the body's likely to be released.

'But as I understand it, Mr Flint's body has already been released in the official sense, and the coroner's just waiting for the funeral to be arranged before he'll let anyone collect it. So it could well be that someone, somewhere, is making funeral arrangements and they're just planning to collect the body nearer the time. No funeral director would want a body like Mr Flint's on the premises for a moment longer than was necessary.'

'Because of security, or because it would tarnish their reputation?' Joanne asked.

'Both.'

'So where might they end up cremating Flint's body then? Tredworth Crematorium in Gloucester and Churston Park in Cheltenham have both said they'll refuse to have him, but I've heard that Gloucestershire Police have advised the solicitor working for Jonathan's two daughters to hold the funeral outside the county anyway.'

'That wouldn't surprise me at all, Joanne. And if that *is* the case, then your guess is as good as mine as to where the funeral will end up being held. Assuming that there is even a funeral to begin with. They might just have him cremated without any ceremony,' Simon said, warming to his act.

'But his ashes could still be returned to his daughters, could they?'

'Yes, if that's what they want. Once Mr Flint's body has been cremated – assuming he *is* going to be cremated – his daughters would still have to decide what should happen with his ashes. But there'd be nothing to stop them from quietly scattering them pretty much wherever they wanted to.'

'So they could still bury his ashes in his parents' grave in Herefordshire then, if they wanted to?'

Although alarmed by the extent of Joanne's knowledge, Simon knew her well enough to know that she would have done her homework and he was quite happy to go on playing the unknowing innocent. 'That's the one option they probably would have problems with.'

'Why?'

'Well, depending on whether Mr Flint's parent's grave is in a churchyard or a local authority cemetery, his daughters would need permission from whoever's in charge of the burial ground before they could bury the ashes there.

'But in Mr Flint's case, even if it was just his ashes there would still be a very real risk of the grave being desecrated, or becoming a morbid tourist attraction; so I'd be quite surprised if the daughters actually got permission to formally bury the ashes.'

'Jonathan Flint's parents are buried in the churchyard of a village called Kings Welham.'

'There you are then,' Simon responded. 'It wouldn't just be a case of putting the ashes into his parents' grave. It would also be about the vicar and the churchwardens having a responsibility to protect the peace and sanctity of the churchyard. And they wouldn't be able to do that if they had ghoulish sightseers trampling over other people's graves so they could see where Flint's ashes were buried.'

'So if it's a churchyard, it's the vicar's job to grant permission, is it?'

'Yes.'

'And you think the vicar would refuse permission for Flint's ashes to be buried there?'

'I can't say for certain. I'm just saying that Mr Flint's notoriety would almost certainly colour the vicar's thinking if he or she had to decide whether or not to grant permission.'

'Thank you, Simon. It's been really helpful talking to you.'

FIVE

'I've got everything I need then, unless there's anything else you're not sure about at the moment?' Simon said.

'No, you've been very thorough, Mr Thorley. Thank you,' Mrs Haskins replied. 'There's a lot to think about, isn't there?'

'There is, yes. But we've only got once chance to get things right, so I need to make sure that I've covered all the bases,' Simon replied apologetically.

'Oh, absolutely. I'm not complaining.' Mrs Haskins reached down for her bag and began putting away her notepad and the document folder she'd been given at the register office. Then, looking up again, she said: 'Actually, there is one other thing. It's rather an odd question I know, but it's been nagging away at me since Dad died and it's something my daughter's curious about too.'

'Try me,' Simon replied, expecting one of the usual questions about whether it really was the person's ashes that you got back; or if he believed in life after death.

'Well ... will someone have to do all this for Jonathan Flint? I mean, he'll have to have a funeral won't he?'

Not for the first time Simon tensed and hoped he wasn't giving himself away.

'Not necessarily. A body has to be lawfully disposed of by burial or cremation, but there's no requirement for there to be any form of ceremony with it. And in fact, it's becoming increasingly common for people to be cremated *without* any ceremony and then for their family to do something with the ashes instead.'

'Really?'

'Yes. We had one family who brought mother down to Gloucestershire to be in a nursing home closer to them; then when she died they had a direct cremation and took her ashes back up north and had a proper church service up there.

'And I've dealt with arrangements for a chap who'd been terminally ill and who wanted a direct cremation so his wife and daughters could spend the money on hiring out the pub where he used to drink and having a big beano to celebrate his life instead.

'So in answer to your question, it's entirely possible that Mr Flint could be cremated without ceremony and his ashes just be quietly scattered somewhere.'

'That would be the sensible thing to do, wouldn't it? My daughter was saying that Facebook is full of people saying he shouldn't be given a proper funeral and that they should just cremate him and tip the ashes away. She said someone was even organising for people to picket the crematorium in Gloucester to prevent him being cremated there!'

'Yes, they were outside the gates when I was conducting a funeral there the other day.'

'They didn't try and stop *you* getting in, did they?'

'Oh, no, they weren't being loud and aggressive or anything like that. They were just making a statement. But it wasn't very nice for my mourners to have that mob staring at them, trying to spot if they might be Jonathan Flint's relatives.'

'Oh, how awful. I'm glad we're going to Cheltenham then.'

'They've had protesters there too. But they've all disbanded now that Gloucester and Cheltenham Councils have said that they'll refuse to handle Mr Flint's cremation. So whatever *does* end up happening, I would imagine it'll take place outside of the county.'

'Maybe they should just bury him out at sea or something,' said Mrs Haskins as she stood up and slung her bag over her shoulder.

'It would certainly solve a lot of problems if they did,' Simon smiled.

'All okay?' Beverley asked, when Simon went back upstairs.

'Yep, fine. Service at Churston Park Crem' and ashes scattered there. No bells and whistles and as long as it's between eleven and two, Mrs Haskins isn't worried what day it is. I wish a few more families were still like that.'

'Funny you should say that. I've had an Alex Turner on the phone. She said you're arranging her father's funeral. That's you-know-who, isn't it?'

'Yes, it is,' Simon replied, feeling a sudden twinge of anxiety. He was keen to meet Alex and Tara anyway, just to see what they were like; but before he could properly set about making funeral arrangements, he needed to establish precisely what their motivations were for wanting to give their father a funeral. 'What did she want?'

'Just to let you know that she's spoken to her sister and that eleven o'clock on Saturday morning is fine. She also said that you *will* be discreet, won't you?!'

Simon gave a mirthless chuckle. 'She needn't worry about that . . .'

*

The headlights of Friday afternoon rush hour traffic flashed past outside as Simon clicked onto Google and typed 'jonathan flint daughters' into the search box. He clicked on an article dated three years previously, written by a journalist who'd covered Flint's trial at Crown Court.

'For a few vivid weeks some seven years ago, the country was captivated by the trial of serial murderer Jonathan Flint and journalists like myself, who were sent to cover the story, were forced to contemplate the vicious and obscene cruelty that Flint had perpetrated against seven – possibly eight – young women who'd fallen into his savage clutches.

'For those of us who were there to observe the proceedings, the horror only ended when the jury foreman announced 'Guilty'. We all breathed a collective sigh of relief and looked forward to returning to reporting on more ordinary crimes.

'But during the trial, taking every bit as prominent a role in the witness stand as the investigating police officers and the various expert witnesses, were Jonathan Flint's two teenage daughters, referred to in court as Daughters 1, we'll call her Ruth, and 2.

'They found themselves having to give an account of the man they'd only ever known as a loving father and as far removed as it was possible to be from the vicious rapist and murderer that everyone else in court had come to know.

'During their time on the witness stand, those two brave girls – neither of whom had ever had the slightest suspicion of their father's sickening crimes – had stared at him with yearning, sorrowful gazes that had belied not anger or betrayal, but simply a bewilderment that was heart-breaking to see.

'In fact, both daughters' vulnerability had capsized everyone who'd been there in court to witness it. Two innocent teenagers who'd stood before us with no defences against the appalling truths they were being confronted with; two teenagers still trying to come to terms with losing their mother to cancer barely a year before their father was arrested.

'The final look that Ruth had given her father in court was a tearful one filled with love and affection; but in the days after she and her sister had finished giving evidence, Ruth was quoted as saying: "People tell me that I'm not to blame for what happened, but I've still got to live with knowing what my father did to those girls."

'And live with it Ruth has.

'She has never had a serious relationship because the spectre of her father's crimes continues to haunt her. She admits her life is, and probably always will be, very lonely; but she fears ending up with someone like her father. Ruth says she will always question her judgement because she still finds it impossible to reconcile her memories of the loving, caring man she knew as her father with the man who was convicted of abducting, raping and killing seven young women during a five-month period in 2007.

'"He was always a very generous and loving father to me and my sister, but it must have been a mask he put on. It's the only way I can think of it," Ruth says. "But when you're a child, you aren't really capable of knowing anyone that well, are you? So when I look back on it now, I wonder if I ever did really know my father.

'"In later times I even began to wonder if my mother had ever suspected anything about him before she died. But despite how much I miss her, I thank God that she wasn't alive to see any of it."

'Ruth was only sixteen when her father's brief reign of terror was ended; and she vividly remembers the night when police officers swarmed into the family home to arrest him on suspicion of multiple counts of murder:

'"It was like having a bomb dropped right into the middle of mine and my sister's lives and into the middle of everything we ever thought we knew about our father," she said.

Ruth spoke of the torment that she and her sister continue to suffer as the daughters of one of the UK's worst serial killers. After their father's arrest, they changed their surname and were helped to start new lives; partly for their own benefit and partly out of a genuine and continuing fear that someone might seek revenge for their father's crimes.

"'Our father sentenced seven young women to death and gave their families and friends a life sentence,' Ruth states, "and he gave me and my sister a life sentence too.

"'I feel like I should be making restitution for his crimes. And because I share my father's DNA it makes me feel dirty and I can't help but wonder if that evil is something that's now a part of me too.

"'I know that I'm not capable of killing anyone; that I'm not a psychopath. But because I'm his daughter I feel like I won't ever be able to live in this world and be a part of it; that I'll always be a spectator, watching normal, more deserving people going about their lives.'"

*

Prestbury Heights, like all new-build housing developments, was an exercise in residential battery farming; and after parking in what he hoped was a communal space, Simon made another check of the property finder map he'd printed off from the internet. He cast furtive glances around him, convinced that from every window he was being watched.

He knew he was being irrational. In a place like this most people probably wouldn't even know who their neighbours were, let alone care who he was, or who he was visiting. But as he locked his car and made his way towards the block where Alex's flat was, he still felt uncomfortably exposed.

Although Simon thought he knew better than to be surprised, Alex Turner – formerly Flint – wasn't at all like he'd imagined when she answered the door.

With auburn, shoulder-length hair, ice-blue eyes and a confident, self-possessed air about her, she was dressed in jeans and a well-fitting Badminton Horse Trials polo shirt, and Simon noticed a pair of the leather country boots so beloved of horsey types tucked behind the door.

He stepped over them and pressed himself against the wall of the tiny hallway so Alex could shut the door again, then followed her up the stairs.

Alex's first-floor flat was small and immaculately tidy. The furniture all matched in a straight-out-the-catalogue kind of way and even the pictures on the walls, which consisted solely of bland photographic images of flowers, seemed to have been chosen to match the colour scheme rather than for their merit as pictures.

The only blot on this clinically well-ordered domestic landscape was the sullen-looking couple occupying the sofa. Carl – presumably – pony-tailed and bearded, was sprawled with his arms across the back of the cream coloured sofa, his legs in a wide 'v' and his feet resting on the heels of well-worn leather boots. Simon couldn't help but feel a pang of anxiety for the pristine carpet.

And then Tara: as unlike her sister as it was possible to be, with long, messy blonde hair that ended in pink-dyed tips, a nose stud and multiple stud earrings.

Of thinner build than Alex, Tara was wearing jeans that, judging by their skin-tight fit and the black panel round the inner thigh area, doubled up as riding breeches, together with a grubby, equestrian-branded gilet. She only had socks on her feet, so Simon figured the country boots at the foot of the stairs were actually hers. Tara had her sister's blue eyes, but none of the self-possession. Instead there was only wariness and, despite the internet article's claims of Alex's vulnerability, it was Tara who looked to be the lost one right then.

After a stilted exchange of greetings Simon seated himself in an armchair and took his folder out of his briefcase. Although his casual tweed jacket, open-neck shirt and beige jeans were a necessary precaution anyway, he felt no less up-tight and on ceremony than if he'd been in a suit. Indeed, judging by Tara and Carl's demeanours, any hopes he might have had of a more casual appearance helping to break down barriers had just been certified dead on arrival.

Alex perched on the other armchair. She didn't offer Simon a drink and he noticed there weren't any used cups in sight. An expectant silence descended and Simon took that as his cue to deploy the opening gambit he'd been rehearsing:

'It goes without saying that I'll do everything I possibly can to ensure that your father's arrangements are handled discreetly and sensitively. But as far as I'm concerned he is still your father and that's how I'll approach things.'

That elicited nothing more than three blank looks, so Simon ploughed on. 'Colin Armstrong has told me that you want your father to be cremated, and he also told me that Gloucestershire Police are advising that –'

'Look mate, we know all this. And about the councils saying they're not prepared to have anything to do with Jonathan's funeral,' Carl put in, his voice gravelly but disconcertingly well-spoken. 'So how about you just cut to the chase and tell us where and when Tara and Alex *can* have their father's funeral?'

'Well, unless you've got anywhere particular in mind yourselves, my suggestion would be to try Lewiston Crematorium in North Avon,' Simon replied, before adding his reasoning.

'So you haven't actually asked them if they'll take Jonathan then?' Carl put in again when Simon had finished.

'No, not yet,' Simon replied, inwardly nettling at Carl's

attitude, particularly as he wasn't even a relative. 'Because of the sensitivities involved, I wanted to meet with you all and establish precisely what it is that you want to have in terms of a funeral for your father before I start making approaches to crematoria.'

'It's pretty obvious – we want them to burn his body for us!' Tara said, earning a sharp look from Alex. 'Well that's what crematoriums do: burn people!' Tara volleyed back.

Simon remained politely impassive, but he decided he had the measure of Tara and Carl now. Alex he still wasn't sure about. 'As I understand it, it's just going to be the three of you there, so do you want there to be a proper service led by a minister? Or would you rather have something more informal – say, just sitting and listening to a piece of music before the curtains close?'

'We want there to be a proper service if we can have one,' Alex said. 'Have a vicar or someone to say a few words. Will we be allowed to have that at the crematorium?'

'If Lewiston are willing to handle the cremation, then by definition we'll be allowed to have a service there too. Although obviously it would be wise to keep it as simple and low-key as possible.'

'That's all we want anyway,' Alex said evenly.

'So are you going to ask this place if we can go there, then?' Tara added plaintively.

'Yes, absolutely. Now that I know what you've got in mind I'll speak to them first thing on Monday and see what they have to say. And if for any reason it is a "no" from them, then I'll just keep working in a wider circle until I find a crematorium that *is* willing.'

'You'll have to, won't you?' Carl shot back.

'But whether it's Lewiston or anywhere else,' Simon continued patiently, 'it's very likely that they'll insist on us having either an early morning or a late afternoon booking, to keep us separate from other services.'

'Yeah, we wouldn't want to spoil anyone else's funeral, would we?' Tara muttered.

Alex shot her sister another withering look, but Simon had to suppress a smile and he suddenly found himself warming to Tara. Had they been any other family he would already have been feeling irritated by now, but the uniqueness of Alex and Tara's situation made it easy to be indulgent towards them.

Alex turned to Simon again.

'We know we've got to keep a low profile and we certainly don't want to disrupt other people's funerals. But I'd prefer it if it was early in the morning anyway.'

'Why?' Tara demanded.

'So it isn't hanging over us all day,' Alex replied.

'But if we're going to have to travel to wherever it is, we won't want an early morning slot will we?'

'You won't get a choice anyway,' Carl chipped in again. 'Those places are like conveyor belts and they sure as hell won't be falling over themselves to do any favours for someone like Jonathan.'

'Carl's got a point. It could well be a case of having to take what we're offered,' Simon responded, glad to be able to agree with Carl about something. 'But once I *have* got a crematorium lined up – whether it's Lewiston or anywhere else, I'll book the soonest sensible date that I can.'

He thought of the increasingly narrow and specific scheduling requirements that families presented him with nowadays; and how even a loved one's funeral was something that had to be shoehorned into people's busy lives. He was sure that was one of the driving factors behind the increasing sense of disillusionment he was feeling towards his job.

'When d'you think that'll be?' Tara asked.

'I'm hoping it'll be the early part of next week. I just need a sensible amount of time to arrange collection of your father's body and get all the documentation delivered to the crematorium; and also to give time for whoever's going to lead the service or ceremony to be able to plan that side of things with you.

'Which leads me on to my next question: would you like it to be a religious service or a non-religious one?'

'Dad wasn't religious at all,' Alex began. 'He—'

'He used to talk to the prison chaplain a lot,' Tara cut in, but it was Alex's use of the word 'Dad' that was still ringing in Simon's ears.

'Only because the chaplain was one of the few people that Dad *could* talk to,' Alex replied. 'You know as well as I do that he didn't actually believe in God.'

She turned to Simon again. 'We can't exactly expect someone to stand there and talk about his life anyway, can we?'

'Not in *that* sense perhaps. But you can still have someone there to lead the service. As I say, you've got the choice to have either a religious service with a minister, or a wholly non-religious ceremony led by a humanist officiant. Or in the big grey area in between, there's the option to have an independent celebrant if you want there to be some spiritual content, but without it being a full-blown religious service.

'The humanist and independent celebrants I work with are all trained professionals, so you'd still have someone leading a proper funeral ceremony for you, whichever way you choose to go.'

'Why not just get the prison chaplain to do it?' Carl said impatiently.

'Because I don't want anyone from the prison. I've had enough of all that,' Alex said firmly. 'I think we should go with a non-religious funeral. What was it you said – a humanitarian service?'

'Humanist ceremony,' Simon replied.

'Dad would have wanted there to be prayers or something though. Like Mum had,' Tara said, her eyes finally starting to redden with tears.

Simon felt a pang of sympathy for her and it frustrated him that neither Alex nor Carl made any effort even just to reach a hand across to her.

'But this isn't like it was for Mum, is it?' Alex responded. 'Her funeral *had* to be held in the church in Westoncote because so many people wanted to come.' Turning to Simon again, she added, 'What about an independent celebrant then? You say they could put something together for us if we just want some prayers included?'

'Yes, absolutely. They take a blank slate approach and build the ceremony entirely around the person who's died, and around whatever elements their family want to include.'

'So Alex and Tara would have to meet one of these celebrants then, and tell them what they want, would they?' Carl asked.

'Ideally, yes. It always helps the celebrant to meet with you if they can, just so they can get a proper sense of things and make sure the ceremony's exactly what you want or need it to be,' Simon replied, glancing at the three of them in turn. 'There's always something that comes out of those meetings that helps to make the funeral more meaningful and personal.'

'I think meaningful and personal would be a challenge in our case. Eleven years ago we found out that we'd never really known our father at all. And that was on top of just losing our mother,' Alex said.

'Yes ...' Simon, lowered his voice respectfully. 'I'm aware that your mother died not long before your father was first arrested.'

The expression on Alex's face altered ever so slightly and Simon wondered if he'd spoken out of turn. Alex hardly needed reminding that her family history was a matter of public record.

'The church was packed for Mum's funeral,' she said pensively. 'And we'd probably be planning for loads of people to be at this one too, if Dad had been the man that everyone thought he was.'

'He *was* to the people who knew him. And he was to us,' Tara said firmly, wiping her eyes again. 'We just didn't know that he had another side to him ...'

Alex regarded her sister for a few moments, then turned back to Simon again. 'What else do we need to talk about?'

'After the cremation there'll still be your father's ashes to be thought about,' Simon said automatically, his thoughts still on Tara's remark and on what it must have been like for her and Alex to have experienced the trauma of their father's arrest while still grieving for their mother.

'How soon will we get them?' Tara replied, answering Simon's next question before he'd asked it.

'Ashes are normally available twenty-four hours after cremation. It's my responsibility to collect them from the crematorium, so I'll make sure that's done as quickly as possible; and then you can have them as soon as you wish.'

'And we collect them from your office, do we?' Alex added.

'Normally, yes. But I'd be perfectly happy to deliver them directly to one of you if you wish.'

'No, we'll come and collect them,' Alex replied, glancing at Tara again. 'We'll come over as soon as you've got them.'

'Okay, thank you. Now, as regards transport arrangements on the day—'

'We won't have to follow the hearse all the way to wherever

it is we have to go, will we?' Tara put in again. 'We had to do that with Mum.'

'No, no, not if you don't want to. And to be honest I don't think it would be wise anyway,' Simon responded, already writing 'crem direct' on his arranging sheet. 'The more discreet we are, the better. Which leads me onto what sort of vehicle we should use to transport the coffin.'

'A hearse of course,' Carl said sharply. 'We don't want him just being put in the back of a black van.'

'Yes, I want him going in a proper hearse!' Tara chimed in.

'Absolutely. That's fine,' Simon responded. 'But all I was going to say is that a hearse is a very visible thing and—'

'A crematorium's a very visible thing,' Carl interjected.

'It is. Point taken,' Simon said equably, tilting his hands up from his folder, fingers outstretched. 'But if you *did* want things to be more discreet, then I do have an estate car with blacked-out windows that I could use if you want me to. Just as an insurance against prying eyes, that's all.'

'He's got a point,' Alex spoke up. 'We don't want photos all over the newspapers if they manage to find out about the funeral.'

'They won't *be* finding out about the funeral if it's kept secret, will they?' Tara replied. 'But if we're going to do this, I want to do it properly. We're doing it for Dad, not for the person everyone else knows him as.'

Simon's heartbeat quickened at hearing Tara voice the very same distillation of their situation that he himself had reached. An image of a body in military uniform washing up on a sunlit Spanish beach flickered through his mind and before he had a chance to lose his nerve, he cautiously put forward the idea he'd been mulling over.

Twenty minutes later he glanced over his arrangement sheet: simple/committal service; independent celebrant; ashes back to family a.s.a.p. for private scattering; hearse direct to crem; plain oak veneered coffin; viewing – yes (he hadn't been expecting that); and flowers to be ordered on Alex and Tara's behalf.

Pleased at how receptive Alex and Tara – and even Carl – had been to the idea he'd suggested, Simon dared himself to believe that even in this situation he might actually have succeeded in opening the way for the funeral to be something really quite positive and healing.

'Colin Armstrong will be dealing with the funeral expenses from your father's estate, so the only other thing we need to do is to complete an application for cremation.'

Pulling out a blank form from his folder, Simon performed another of his well-worn recitations: 'It's basically a declaration from you as the next of kin that there was nothing suspicious about your father's death – in the criminal sense,' he lowered his tone momentarily to show that the irony wasn't lost on him, 'and that there's no reason why his body shouldn't be cremated.

'Which one of you shall I put down as the applicant? You've both got equal precedence as the daughters.'

'You can do it,' Tara said, looking at Alex.

'Okay,' Simon said, clicking his biro again as he spoke. 'Can I start by asking your full name then please, Alex?'

When he'd completed the form Simon handed it to Alex for her to sign. Then as he slid it back into his folder again he cast a final glance over his arrangement sheet. 'I've got everything I need then, unless there's anything else you're not sure about at the moment?' He glanced at Alex, Tara and Carl in turn.

'When will you go and get Dad's body?' Tara asked.

'As soon as I've got a crematorium booked, Colin Armstrong will inform the coroner's office and it's at that point that they'll release your father's body.'

SIX

When Simon had entered the funeral trade as a wide-eyed teenager in the mid-1980s, he'd found a profession still firmly rooted in rituals of grief and mourning established in the Victorian era.

Funeral services were almost entirely held in church or at the crematorium and were invariably led by a minister of religion.

Music had been almost the sole preserve of the organist and although the idea of having specific pieces of recorded music had increasingly been gaining traction at crematorium funerals, it had still been very conservative in nature – usually classical pieces, Welsh male-voice choirs and military bands. 'Stairway To Heaven' would still have been a brave choice back then.

But thirty years on, secularism had well and truly broken religion's stranglehold on funerals and the role of the priest/minister had been comprehensively usurped by the rise of professional funeral celebrants: a rainbow coalition of avowedly non-religious humanist officiants, blank slate civil and independent celebrants and 'inter-faith ministers' sailing under a self-proclaimed flag of religious convenience.

From tiny beginnings in the early 1990s, when the first few humanist officiants had quietly offered non-religious funeral ceremonies as an alternative to the church's hegemony, the number of 'bespoke funerals' and celebrants offering to conduct them had grown exponentially; and where funeral celebrancy had originally been a pioneering movement, it was now a saturated marketplace.

Reputable, well-established celebrants – vocational in their approach and representing the best of their movement – were having to compete against eager and altruistic newly-trained entrants on the one hand, and one-size-fits-all, standard-script merchants on the other, all trying to wheedle, undercut and hustle their way into funeral directors' phone books.

And therein lay the problem. Despite hopes that the laws of Darwinism would prevail, the reality was that funeral directors were the only filter.

While some, like Simon, would only allow the best celebrants anywhere near their families, and would willingly battle with mismatching diaries to achieve this, too many funeral directors simply defaulted to the first celebrant who answered their phone; or to the one who was free on Wednesday at 11.00 am.

But the fact that Alex and Tara had opted for a celebrant-led ceremony was both a blessing and a challenge. Simon had a coterie of celebrants all just a phone call away, but it wasn't enough just to know whether a family required a humanist, a civil/independent, or even a dog collar for hire. (He had a couple of retired priests he could call on if a family wanted religion without all the encumbrances of using their local parish priest).

People-matching was key to Simon's approach and that meant there was only one celebrant he had in mind to use: Marie Sandbrook, a Cheltenham-based civil and undoubtedly one of the best of her kind. His only reservation about approaching Marie was that he would be putting her in the same position that Colin Armstrong had put him in; although as a celebrant Marie would be unlikely to suffer any damage to her own reputation by conducting Flint's funeral.

If she did ever find herself having to justify her involvement, she could truthfully claim that she'd been approached by a funeral director with whom she worked regularly and that the ceremony had not been intended to honour Flint in any way, but simply to provide words of solace and comfort for his two innocent daughters.

The dilemma lay in Marie's unswerving commitment to the needs of each family she worked with; and how, by the very nature of her role and her heartfelt approach to it, she would have to broach considerably more personal and uncomfortable matters with Alex and Tara than Simon had needed to. And would it be fair to expose her to what that might entail?

This was one of those occasions when the standard-issue Church of England funeral came into its own. The Bible had something for all occasions of course, and in circumstances like this, quoting from the scriptures would have been a perfectly valid means of addressing the unspeakable.

But having agreed – not unwillingly – to take the funeral on, Simon had become fiercely possessive of his controversial commission. After all, he hadn't just been granted a walk-on part in criminal history; he would have a hand in writing it; and by appointing a celebrant of his own choosing he could at least retain some creative control over Flint's obsequies. Where ministers of religion were a law unto themselves, celebrants were sub-contractors.

After mentally composing his entrée, he made the call, only to find himself listening to Marie's voicemail message.

'Hello Marie, it's Simon Thorley. I'm hoping you can help me with a funeral please, so if you could call me back when you're able, that would be great. Thank you.'

Simon logged on to the internet again, checking for any new

articles about Flint's death. He was still anxious about the possibility of Alex's neighbours knowing who she really was and that having spotted a stranger visiting at the weekend they might quite correctly have surmised that matters were afoot.

But relieved to find that there was nothing new online, he once again reverted back to one of the existing articles, this time just to remind himself of precisely what *was* in the public domain before he made his next phone call.

Leaving the article open on his computer screen, Simon dialled the number.

'Good morning, Lewiston Crematorium.'

'Hi Alison, it's Simon Thorley. Is there any chance I could speak to Rob please? Thank you.'

A short silence ensued as the call was transferred, then: 'Hi, Simon.'

'Hi Rob. I've ... erm, got an enquiry to make and it's a bit of an awkward one, so can we treat this as a confidential conversation please?'

'Course we can. How can I help?'

'I've been asked to arrange a very sensitive funeral and I'm wondering whether Lewiston would be willing to handle it for us. The deceased is Jonathan Flint.'

'Oh ... right ... That *is* a bit sensitive.' Rob fell silent for a moment. 'What would you be looking at? A full service, or just a committal?'

'It would just be a very small ceremony. There's only going to be three people attending – two immediate relatives and the partner of one of them. They want a celebrant to lead it, but as I say, it would only be a very short ceremony. And obviously the intention would be to hold it in complete secrecy.'

'So is this a private arrangement then, or is it being done under a council contract or something?'

'No, it's private arrangement. There's a solicitor handling

things, but rather unfortunately for me it just so happens that the solicitor is one that we work with quite regularly, hence why the funeral's come my way. But I have also met with the immediate family.

'Anyway, the reason I'm calling you is that Gloucestershire Police have advised the family to hold the funeral outside the county, and the two councils that run the two crems we've got here in Gloucestershire have just issued a statement saying they'll refuse the use of their crematoria and cemeteries, out of respect for public feeling in the county. So it's been left to me to find a suitable alternative.'

'I saw from the press reports that Jonathan Flint had two daughters,' Rob said. 'It must be an awful situation for them. And it's obviously a difficult one for you. On the one hand you've got the daughters to look after, and on the other you've got your reputation to think about.'

'Tell me about it,' Simon responded.

'But everyone's entitled to have a funeral I suppose – regardless of what they've done in life,' Rob continued. 'And it's not our place to make moral judgements, is it? But there are other factors that would have to be taken into consideration with one like this.'

'Exactly,' Simon agreed, content to be patient with Rob's stalling. He knew the final decision probably wouldn't be Rob's to make anyway. Lewiston Crematorium was part of a national group and something like this was likely to need passing up the management chain.

'Will there be police guarding the funeral or anything like that?' Rob asked.

'I don't know yet. Gloucestershire Police want to be kept informed so they can liaise with the force for the area where the funeral ends up taking place, so I suppose it's possible that there might be a discreet presence.

'But it's in everyone's interests to get this funeral done as quickly and quietly as possible. Just have a little ceremony for the daughters like they've asked for, and then slide off again without anyone being any the wiser,' Simon added.

'Speaking for myself, I wouldn't necessarily have a problem with the funeral taking place here, Simon. If it's done in secrecy and at the right time of day then it wouldn't necessarily need to affect anyone else.

'But my big worry is that if word *does* get out before the funeral takes place, then we could run into problems. If it finds its way onto social media or something, we could have people turning up and creating all kinds of security risks – not just to you and Mr Flint's family, but to other families and to our staff too. So I think for something like this I'd need to speak to our managing director.'

'Sure. I understand.'

'I'll call you back as soon as I can, Simon. But rest assured I'll make sure this is kept confidential.'

'Thank you, Rob.'

Simon put the phone down and immediately began looking up the websites of other crematoria within a reasonable distance. He had a feeling he would need to.

'Rob Howard for you,' Beverley called out half an hour later.

Simon tensed. 'Hello again, Rob.'

'Hello, Simon. I've spoken to our MD. He's got the same concerns that I have: that no matter how discreetly everything's handled, there's still a danger that word of the funeral could leak out – particularly as we're only just over the border from Gloucestershire anyway. Our MD's already heard about the people picketing Gloucester and Cheltenham Crems and he doesn't want to risk that happening here.

'I'm really sorry. I've never had to turn a funeral away before and I'm not doing it now simply because it's Jonathan

Flint. We're here to provide a public service and we wouldn't normally turn anyone away, but our MD just thinks that in Mr Flint's case there's just too much risk of disruption to other families.'

'No, that's fine, Rob. I totally understand. I wouldn't want your other funerals to be put at risk of disruption any more than you would. But thank you for your time on this anyway. I'll set to work on finding a Plan B.'

'Like I said, I'm really sorry I can't help you with this, Simon,' Rob replied. 'But good luck with it all the same.'

'D'you think we're going to get a lot of that?' Beverley said when Simon put the phone down again.

'I bloody hope not,' he sighed. But enquiries with two council-run crematoria that he'd previously conducted funerals at in neighbouring Wiltshire both yielded refusals on the grounds that two of the murders had occurred in the county.

Calls to Attwood and Bromsgrove Crematoriums in Worcestershire also drew negative responses: 'We've already had people phoning up because we're the nearest crematorium to High Marston Prison,' said the manager at Attwood, 'and we've even had reporters pretending to be mourners and then approaching our staff to ask if Jonathan Flint is going to be cremated here.'

At Bromsgrove matters had escalated further: 'One chap whose mother's funeral is due to be held here got quite abusive and accused us of a cover-up when we told him we weren't handling Jonathan Flint's cremation,' Simon was told.

He wasn't particularly surprised, but he couldn't help feeling annoyed and frustrated at how crematoria which all had to host unwholesome funerals on occasion, were reluctant to host a brief and determinedly discreet service for a convicted murderer.

The phone rang again as Beverley was preparing to go down to the bank. 'Marie Sandbrook for you,' she called out, before shrugging on her coat.

Simon's mood lightened slightly as he picked up his phone again. 'Hello Marie. Thanks for calling back.' He gave a thumbs up sign to Beverley as she headed out the door.

'No problem. You've got a funeral for me?'

'Hopefully ... yes. You know how I always throw you the curve ball jobs? The split families, the suicides, and the ones who want a pagan funeral followed by a Viking-style cremation complete with misty lake and burning boat?'

Marie chuckled. 'And every time we cope with what's thrown at us and manage to create something worthwhile. So what is it this time?'

'Jonathan Flint.'

There was a pause. 'You're not joking are you?'

'No, I'm afraid I'm not.'

'Oh Simon ...' Marie sighed. 'How did it come your way?'

'Turns out that a solicitor we deal with regularly is Flint's executor. Flint's got two daughters, but they asked the solicitor to oversee the arrangements, so it's found its way to my door.'

'And the daughters want to have a ceremony, do they?'

'Of sorts, although I suspect we'll be looking more towards a 'full committal' type of thing. I met the daughters at the weekend and obviously there were various things that came up. But basically they just want there to be a simple little ceremony with three of them in attendance, at a crematorium yet to be decided upon; and all done in conditions of absolute secrecy.'

'I heard that Tredworth and Churston Park are refusing to handle it and I saw all those silly people outside the gates at Tredworth the other day,' Marie said.

'Oh, don't get me started about them,' Simon replied. 'We've got social media to thank for that nonsense. But Tredworth and Churston Park were never on the cards anyway. It would have been madness, not to mention utterly insensitive, to try using either of them; but the solicitor's already had Gloucestershire Police leaning on him to have the funeral held outside the county anyway.

'However, the way things are going, we might end up having to go further afield than even I was expecting. I've already been turned down by Lewiston, Kingslow and Lydiard in Wiltshire and Attwood and Bromsgrove in Worcestershire.'

'Honestly?'

Simon recounted his conversations with the various crematorium managers, then added: 'I'm not really selling this to you, am I?'

'Not really!' Marie replied. 'But strangely enough, I was talking to another celebrant at Tredworth yesterday about whether either of us would be prepared to take on Jonathan Flint's funeral if we were approached.'

'And did you reach a verdict on which you were both agreed?' Simon asked.

Marie gave a reluctant-sounding sigh. 'I said that I'd refuse to do it. I'm so sorry, Simon.' She sounded tearful. 'I never dreamt it would come my way anyway, but there's just no way I would ever consider doing it. I haven't told anyone else this before, but I knew one of the girls that he murdered: Lucy Heaton. Back when I was nursing I worked alongside Lucy's mother, Karen. We were good friends – we still are. And I used to babysit for Lucy when she was young.'

'Oh Christ, Marie ... I'm so sorry ...' Simon responded, his insides shrivelling with guilt. 'I had no idea. I feel awful for asking you now, I really do.'

'You haven't done anything wrong, Simon. Honestly, you haven't. You weren't to know. Like I said, I've never told anyone. You're the first one to know. But I'm going to put the phone down now if you don't mind, because you'll need to be finding someone who can help you and it's risky enough for you to be talking about this over the phone as it is.'

'Marie?'

'I'll catch up with you soon Simon, I promise.' And with that, Marie hung up.

'Fuck, fuck, fuck...' Simon muttered, bitterly regretting his quip about 'curve ball jobs'. It was true: there wasn't any way that he could have known about Marie's connection with Lucy Heaton; but that didn't make him feel any better right then.

For Marie to have been there alongside Lucy's mother and experience the trauma of... well, it didn't bear thinking about.

Simon resolved to let the dust settle for a day or two and then catch up with her again to smooth things over. Marie was far too professional for something like this to come between them, and she did at least know the reasons why he was doing the funeral; but it was another stark reminder, if one were even needed, of just what was at stake in all this.

Meanwhile the clock was still ticking and every moment of delay between now and the moment when Flint's coffin was finally committed to the flames would only increase the risk of the arrangements being exposed.

Simon spun round in his chair and reached for the office phone directory. There was only one other celebrant he was prepared to turn to now that Marie was out of the equation: Philip Coleridge, a humanist celebrant with an equally vocational approach to his work and a similar level of experience to Marie. He also just happened to live more locally than she did. To Simon's utter relief Philip answered his phone straight away.

Simon delivered a tactful reworking of his opening lines and then came clean about his abortive approach to Marie. He didn't elaborate on her reasons for refusing, other than that they extended well beyond a simple reluctance to conduct the funeral of someone like Flint.

'I never imagined I might be faced with something like this when I first trained as a celebrant,' Philip said after listening patiently. 'But then, if you and I were to sit in judgement on all the people who come our way, we probably wouldn't do half the funerals that we do. We just have to put ourselves outside of all that, find a way to honour each person who's died and create the best outcome that we can for their family.

'But at least with something like this you know what you're dealing with. I mean, if you think about it we could both have done funerals in the past for people who've been guilty of terrible things without us even knowing about it.'

'Yeah, absolutely,' Simon agreed. He'd been thinking exactly the same thing since meeting Alex and Tara. *There would probably have been loads of people for Dad's funeral too, if he'd been the man that everyone always thought he was.*

'But on the strength of what you're telling me, Simon, then other than natural caution I can't really see that I've got any reasonable grounds for refusing to do this one, particularly as Marie has already turned you down.

'Whatever her reasons are though – and I'm sure they're very good ones – I'm quite glad that she's chosen to spare herself. But blimey, Simon, you've really thrown down the gauntlet this time ...' Philip gave a loud sigh. 'Go on, I'll say yes. I'll do it. We've done some good work together in the past, so let's see what we can pull out the bag with this one. It'll be an experience if nothing else.'

'Thank you, Philip, I appreciate it. I really do.'

'What can you tell me at the moment?'

'It's Flint's solicitor who's ultimately responsible for the arrangements, but as you're probably aware, Flint has two daughters and the solicitor asked me to speak to them to see if I could get a sense of what it is they're actually hoping for in terms of a funeral.

'I met with them on Saturday morning and I've got a pretty clear idea now of where they're at in terms of their relationship with their father and what they want the funeral to be.

'But in the meantime, the coroner won't release the body until he's received assurances from the solicitor that a funeral director has been appointed and that a date and time has been booked at a crematorium – and that's the next challenge.'

Simon repeated the account of all the refusals he'd had. 'So to be absolutely honest, I'm wondering where to try next.'

'How far are you prepared to travel?' Philip asked.

'To wherever I can find a crem' that'll have us,' Simon responded.

'I did a funeral at Llancroes Crematorium in South Wales recently and I was really impressed with the place. The staff there were excellent. But the reason I mention it is that the family were from Gloucester and Walkers were the FD's and they actually travelled down there in cortege.

'So if they managed it, then Llancroes has to be worth thinking about for Flint, doesn't it?'

'Yes, it does,' Simon agreed. 'And if they're all the way down in South Wales then they might not have quite so many qualms about accepting Flint either . . .'

'Exactly.'

'D'you know Philip, the more I think about it, the more I like the idea. Like you said, it's not really that far to travel given the circumstances. But by crossing the river into Wales there is that extra degree of separation to it all.'

'It's got to be worth a try, Simon. And Llancroes is local authority-run, so they shouldn't have too many worries about their reputation either – especially if it's going to be done in secret. And I'd certainly be happy to go down there again – particularly for one like this,' Philip added.

'Okay, thank you. I'll give them a call then and see what they say,' Simon said, feeling like sunlight might finally be breaking through the clouds.

'And what's the story with the daughters?' Philip continued. 'They had to be given new identities after their father was convicted, didn't they? So do they still live in the county?'

'One's in Ross-on-Wye and the other one's in Cheltenham.'

'How were they when you met them?'

'Now there hangs a tale. They're both very different as sisters, but they seem to be singing from the same hymn sheet. It'll just be the two of them at the funeral. Along with the partner of one of them, unfortunately.'

'Oh? How so?'

'It's nothing controversial. It's just that the partner wasn't a very helpful or supportive presence on Saturday, that's all. But after listening to what the daughters themselves had to say, I really think that if you and I can play our cards right then there's a chance here for us to be able to snatch something really quite honourable from the jaws of Jonathan's dishonour.'

'Gosh, that's very poetic, Simon! I'm intrigued.'

'I'd rather not say too much more on the phone; and I don't want to risk an email either, just in case it goes astray. So could I arrange to call round and talk it through with you in person?'

'You don't have to call round – I'm perfectly happy to come to the office. Or would you prefer to talk off the premises?'

'No, it's not that. I just think it would be safer to talk in person, that's all. But if you're happy to come here, then so much the better.'

'I haven't got much on tomorrow, so give me a time and I'll be there.'

'How about first thing then? Say nine o'clock, just in time for the first kettle-boiling of the day.'

'Excellent idea!'

'Thank you, Philip. I really do appreciate this. And while I've got you on then, can you just give me your availability for the next couple of weeks? Then between now and tomorrow morning I'll plead my case with Llancroes and see if I can get something arranged.'

'Sure. Let me just get my diary. I'll need a whole day for this one. Quite apart from the distance, I won't have the headspace for anything else.'

'No, I can't imagine you would. I'll be perfectly happy to organise transport for you though, if you don't want the hassle of driving.

'And don't worry about charging whatever you want either. The solicitor knows there may have to be extra charges because of the nature of the funeral, but that's all fine with him. The estate's going to be picking up the tab anyway.'

'Jonathan Flint's last gift to the taxpayer then?' said Philip. 'That's something I suppose.'

SEVEN

Llancroes Crematorium's website was unusually detailed, and Simon carefully studied each page. He switched to Google Maps to examine the layout of the site and Street View to gauge how much privacy and seclusion it would actually offer.

Llancroes appeared to be a typical post-war crematorium, but no worse for being so. Indeed, it looked considerably better laid out than Gloucester's hopelessly outdated Tredworth Crematorium, which was so cramped and unfit for purpose that there was absolutely no privacy to be had outside of the chapel itself.

Clicking on the 'Contact Us' page, Simon dialled the number shown and after asking to speak to the registrar-manager, he found himself listening to a broad Welsh accent.

'Hello... Mr *Thorley*, is it? This is Diane Roberts. How can I y'elp?'

'Um, bit of a delicate matter, so I'm approaching you in confidence, if I may please.'

He got an efficient-sounding 'Right you are' in response.

'I've been asked to arrange a very sensitive funeral, and I'm wondering whether Llancroes Crematorium would be willing to help me with it. The deceased is Jonathan Flint.'

'Jonathan Flint is it? That *is* a sensitive funeral then. And there's to be a service beforehand, is there? Or is it just a committal you're wanting?'

'No, the family want there to be a small ceremony, but there'll only be three of them in attendance. And obviously we'd be looking to do it all in complete secrecy.'

'I'm sure. And may I ask what brings you in our direction? Only we 'ad a funeral from Gloucester down y'ere just recently.'

'Yes, it was the humanist officiant who conducted that funeral who suggested I speak to you. He said how helpful and friendly you'd all been and how travelling down from Gloucester had all worked easily enough.'

'Was that Mr Coleridge?'

'That's him.'

'Yes, I remember him. Nice chap. Very caring and efficient. We get all sorts of celebrants y'ere nowadays and not all of them are as professional as they should be.'

'No, I can imagine. We have the same problem up our way.'

'And Mr Coleridge is going to be doing Mr Flint's funeral is he?'

'He is, yes.'

'So 'ave you actually approached any crematoria closer to where you are?'

Simon recited the story once more.

'You've 'ad quite a time of it then.'

'I certainly have.'

'So you're approaching us because we're the next furthest away then?'

'That and the fact that because you're over in South Wales I don't think anyone would suspect the funeral being held there. And as I said, Philip Coleridge has become something of a fan after his visit to you.'

'That's nice to y'ear! It's true though, we probably are far enough away from Gloucestershire to make this a sensible place to 'ave the funeral. Tell me though, is there likely to be a police presence or anything like that?'

'Gloucestershire Police have asked to be kept informed of where the funeral will be held, so they can inform the relevant local force, but there hasn't been any specific mention of a security presence or anything like that as yet.

'But I can assure you that my sole intention – and indeed that of the family – is simply to find a willing crematorium somewhere outside of Gloucestershire, hold a quiet little ceremony and then disappear again without anyone ever knowing that we've been there.'

'That's 'alf the battle, isn't it?' Diane said. 'It's not just about keeping the funeral itself quiet: it's about what 'appens afterwards if people get to know where Mr Flint was cremated. They'll be fretting about their loved one being cremated in the same place as a murderer and all that sort of thing. I'm not trying to be melodramatic, but you know what I mean.'

'I know exactly what you mean,' Simon said, anxious to know which way this conversation was going.

'Okay, Mr Thorley, I'll tell you what I'm goin' to do ... I'm going to say yes. And if anyone asks, then I want it said that I'm agreeing to it purely on y'umanitarian grounds. But I need you to promise me that every effort will be made to keep the funeral as low-key as possible.'

'You have my word on that,' Simon said, almost euphoric with relief. 'And thank you. It's extremely generous of you and I appreciate it. I really do.'

'I'll need to run this past my manager at the county council mind, and then get back to you about exactly 'ow we *do* go about doing it. I've certainly got some conditions in mind. But as I say, in principle I'm prepared to have it y'ere.'

'Then that's a huge weight off my mind. And thank you again. I'll have to break it to the family that they'll be having a trip to South Wales; but quite honestly they'll just need to be as grateful as I am that you're willing to handle the funeral for us.'

'Well, we can't all be dog-in-the-manger about it, can we? I can well understand why the other crematoria have turned it down, but it's still got to be done somewhere. You can't just go and drop Mr Flint in the sea, although I'm sure there's probably lots of people out there who'd be 'appy if you did.'

*

Philip Coleridge, a university lecturer prior to his reinvention in early retirement as a humanist officiant, was comfortably dressed in cord trousers and a jumper. 'Ah, wonderful! Thank you,' he said, peering over his retro-style, half-moon spectacles as Beverley came into the interview lounge and put two mugs of coffee down on the little table. He waited for her to shut the door again behind her. 'So we're going to Llancroes then?'

'We are,' Simon replied. 'Diane Roberts spoke to her superiors at the county council and mercifully they've agreed.'

'That's great. I was really impressed with Diane and her team. She's definitely one of life's no-nonsense types, but that's no bad thing for something like this. I think we'll be as safe down there as anywhere.' Philip opened his diary. 'Have you got a date and time fixed?'

'Yes. Easter's already starting to clog up the crem's diary, so I've had to go for Wednesday eleventh of April at four o'clock,' Simon replied. 'Is four o'clock going to be okay for you?'

'Yes. That's fine. Better than I was expecting actually. I had visions of having to leave home at silly o'clock in the morning to do a nine or a nine-thirty.'

'So did I. But Diane wants us there at the end of the day when everyone else has gone.'

'I've still got to square that with the daughters and the

solicitor though – not that they've got much choice. But I haven't had a chance to speak to any of them yet. And I've also got to break the news to the solicitor about the crem' fees...'

'Has Diane bumped them up then?'

'Not like that, no. But she's made it a condition that we book and pay for the three and the three-thirty as well, to guarantee a buffer zone. Apparently it's an arrangement they've used once before, when they had to partition off another funeral that was a bit controversial.'

Philip shook his head admiringly. 'She's got it all sussed, hasn't she?'

'Certainly has.' Simon chuckled. 'I'd have snatched her hand off just to have a begrudging 'yes' and an early morning slot, so I can see why you liked it down there. Thank you for recommending it. You've really saved my bacon.'

'Glad I could help. Okay, so ... Wednesday eleventh of ... April ... at four o'clock.' Philip wrote it down. Then, putting his diary to one side again, he said: 'You won't believe this, but there was a discussion on the celebrants' forum that I belong to last night, about whether any of them would have been willing to conduct Jonathan Flint's funeral if they'd been asked.'

'Were you left cursing me for handing you the poisoned chalice then?' Simon asked, still haunted by his ill-fated approach to Marie Sandbrook.

'No, of course not. You only did the asking. I was the mad fool who said yes.' Philip rolled his eyes and smiled. 'But it was rather surreal to be sat there watching the discussion unfold. I dropped a few pebbles in the water to see where the ripples went, and it was really quite revealing to see what the other celebrants had to say.'

'Which was?'

'Well, opinion was very divided, as you'd expect. One

celebrant said she'd do it if she was paid a massively inflated fee but, needless to say, she was given pretty short shrift. And another one said she would have turned it down because of the risk to her personal safety, which was understandable.

'But some of them were wondering whether as celebrants we should draw a line and say that because Jonathan Flint is *so* notorious, it would be too inappropriate to conduct a bespoke ceremony for him. One chap even thought it would be better if the funeral was conducted by a priest, because then the focus could at least be put on passing Flint back to God for judgement or forgiveness!

'I ask you, what kind of attitude is that from a celebrant?! Just downright laziness. If they genuinely don't feel able to cope with a situation as extreme as this – and there'd be no shame in a good celebrant saying that – then they should just politely decline on the grounds of making way for someone who does feel strong enough to tackle it.'

Philip leant forward. 'Incidentally, I'm not having a dig at Marie Sandbrook when I say that. Whatever her reasons were, I'm sure they were very good ones and I respect that.'

'I know you do. And she most certainly does have good reasons,' Simon replied. 'But did anyone on your forum have any useful thoughts to offer in the end?'

'Most of them felt the same as me: that if the ceremony doesn't actually do anything to *honour* Flint, but simply sets out to bring comfort and closure to his daughters, then that would outweigh all the controversy surrounding it.'

'I'm glad you and I aren't the only ones who see it that way,' Simon said with feeling. 'We *are* only doing this for Alex and Tara. There wouldn't even be a funeral if they weren't asking for one. And you're still okay about doing it?'

'Of course I am,' Philip replied. 'Don't worry about me.'

'Thank you,' Simon said, with a tight-lipped smile. 'At least there's one thing we can be sure of: it won't be a celebration-of-life ceremony.'

'No, absolutely not,' Philip murmured. 'But there might still be something in Flint's life from the times before he committed his crimes that we can find to honour. His daughters never had the faintest idea what was going on, did they? From what I can gather after looking it all up on the internet last night, they'd always regarded him as a wonderful, caring father, so maybe that part of his life really was genuine.'

'That was pretty much the sense I got from them. Although how you'd go about weaving that into a ceremony, I don't know. And I might just have made it even more complicated now that I've put my suggestion for the funeral to the daughters...'

'Yes, what is this mystery idea of yours? I thought that was a wonderful phrase of yours: "snatching something honourable from the jaws of Jonathan's dishonour." I hope you don't mind, but I conjured an excuse to quote that on the forum last night. I didn't say where it came from of course, but it went down really well with the other celebrants.'

Simon explained what it was he'd put to Alex and Tara and to his relief even Philip seemed genuinely taken with the idea. 'And they're still undecided about music at the moment?' he asked.

'Yes. In fairness, they're both very alert to the fact that if we do have music then we'll need to be very careful about what it is. But they do also agree that it'll be very cold and austere if there isn't *something*,' Simon replied.

'Alex, the eldest daughter, mentioned that she inherited her mother's collection of eighties music, but she didn't think there was anything suitable in amongst that. So I took the liberty of saying that you might be able to suggest something suitable. Although quite what would constitute 'suitable' in this situation, heaven only knows.'

'I'm sure I can help them come up with something,' Philip said. He leant back in his chair and gave a loud sigh. 'We'll never do another funeral like this, will we?'

'No, we won't,' Simon agreed solemnly. 'We really won't.'

'Anyway, what do you want me to do about making contact with them?' Philip asked.

'I'll give you Alex's details,' Simon picked up his arranging folder from the coffee table. 'She's the one taking charge now. But let me break the news to her that we're looking at a trip to South Wales first, then I'll call you and give you the green light to get in contact with her yourself.'

*

'Hello?'

'Hello Alex, it's Simon Thorley – from Arthur Williams and Son. Is it okay to talk for a moment?'

'Yes, it's fine.'

'Okay, well, I've finally been able to get a crematorium lined up. I've done the absolute best I can, but I'll be honest, it hasn't panned out quite how I'd imagined.'

'So it won't be at that Lewisham place or whatever it's called then?'

'Lewiston. No. Unfortunately they've turned us down.' Simon gave a tactful rendering of the now-familiar story.

'My father's body is only going to one of these places to be burnt, for God's sake! Are they worried he's going to come back and haunt them afterwards or something?'

'I don't know, Alex. The risk of disruption to other people's funerals is one thing. But you're right: the actual business of hosting the ceremony and carrying out the cremation would be no different to any other funeral.'

'But you've found somewhere that *will* take us?' Alex said more calmly.

'Yes ...' Simon braced himself. 'A crematorium in South Wales has agreed to have us.'

'South Wales?!'

'Yes. The celebrant I've approached has just done a funeral at a crematorium down there and he was very impressed with the place. Apparently the person who'd died was from Gloucester, but the family wanted to use that particular crematorium and, despite the distance, it all worked out very smoothly. So I spoke to the crematorium manager and she's agreed to have us "on humanitarian grounds", to quote her precise words.'

'On humanitarian grounds ...' Alex repeated softly. 'So we've got to take my father's body all the way to South Wales just to get it cremated?'

'Unless we're prepared to travel even further afield, then ... yes, I'm afraid we will.'

'I'm going to have a hell of a job telling Tara that,' Alex said, sounding defeated. 'But we need to get this over with and get on with our lives. Have you got a date for the funeral then?'

Bracing himself again, Simon said: 'We're looking at Wednesday the eleventh of April, at four o'clock. I know you wanted it sooner than that, but the manager made it a condition that as well as having the last booking of the day, we also block-book the previous two slots, to ensure a buffer zone from any other funerals. So the eleventh of April was the first date the crematorium diary could accommodate that.'

'Wednesday, eleventh of April at four 0'clock,' Alex repeated, sounding as if all the fight truly had gone out of her now. 'Okay, I've written that down. I'll try and explain all that to Tara then.'

'Thank you. And I'm really sorry to ask even more of you, but could you phone me back as soon as you *have* spoken to

Tara please, just so that I can get everything confirmed and get things moving for you.'

It was two long hours before Alex called back, but Simon got his reward: 'Tara's agreed to it all.'

'Thank you, Alex.' He didn't want to imagine what Tara's reaction had been, but that wasn't his problem.

He went on to explain that Philip Coleridge was the 'independent' celebrant lined up to take the ceremony and that Philip would be making contact now that the arrangements were confirmed. And although that second conversation with Alex marked the point of no return, Simon still felt as if an enormous weight had been lifted from his shoulders when he put the phone down.

His next two calls were to Philip and then to Colin Armstrong, who sounded as pleased and relieved as Simon was.

'I must confess I never expected that you'd end up having to go as far as South Wales,' Armstrong said. 'But as you say, perhaps it's not such a bad thing. I'll inform the coroner's office right away.'

With the date and time finally set, notifications would soon begin trickling through to various third parties and Simon knew that the secrecy of the arrangements would no longer be his to command. There was almost nothing he could now do to prevent the risk of someone, somewhere, leaking information about the funeral – whether by accident or by design.

He tried to think of all the scenarios in which that might occur, and his thoughts quickly leapt from the release of Flint's body being mentioned in some routine channel of communication between the coroner's office and their local media in Worcestershire, through to an altogether more imaginative, but no less likely scenario whereby a pillow-talk remark from a crematorium technician might find its way onto his wife's Facebook page.

*

Simon had called at Philip Coleridge's home – a lovingly maintained cottage in a village a couple of miles from Bybrook – numerous times, but he'd never actually set foot inside; and judging by the furnishings and the craftsman-built kitchen that he now found himself in, it was clear that Philip and his wife had invested a great deal of time and money into the place.

'Tea, coffee or something stronger?' Philip asked.

'Tea, thank you.'

'Sure?'

'Yes, thanks. One sniff of the barman's apron and I'm anyone's otherwise.'

Philip chuckled. 'Tea it is then. How d'you like it?'

'Builder's. Two sugars,' Simon replied as Philip switched on the kettle and gathered up a couple of mugs. 'How did you get on then?'

'Well, needless to say, it was one of the more memorable family visits that I've done.'

'Because of who it is, or because of what happened while you were there?'

'Just because of who it is. But I think I've managed to put something together. For security's sake though, I won't email you an advance copy of the script if you don't mind.'

'No, of course. That's fine.'

'And while we're on the subject of "by your leaves", would you mind if we stayed in here? Gill's in the lounge watching one of her programmes on catch-up.'

Simon perched himself on a stool by the kitchen island. It

hadn't occurred to him to wonder what Philip's wife might have felt about her husband's involvement in Flint's funeral, but perhaps he'd just had the answer.

Philip put a mug of tea down in front of him and pulled out another stool. 'I've had to write ceremonies for some right ne'er-do-wells in the past and it's always difficult to know how to go about acknowledging that. You can't just stand there and list a person's misdeeds, unless they've really defined their life in some way.'

'A much-loved husband, son, brother, car thief and scrote,' Simon muttered.

'Exactly!' Philip chuckled again. 'But if they *have* done genuinely bad things, and caused a great deal of hurt and anguish to others, then that has to be acknowledged. And the trouble with that is that you then risk trashing that person's memory and alienating all the mourners.

'The person who's died might well have been a thieving wretch who mugged little old ladies for their pension money; but like you said, he's still going to be a husband, father, son, brother and friend to the people at his funeral, isn't he? So there's a delicate balance to be struck.'

'So does the fact that Flint was responsible for abducting, raping and murdering at least seven young girls and women mean that the challenge of having to strike a balance is removed then?' Simon asked.

'Ironically, it does actually make things a bit easier. His crimes are writ so large that I don't have to worry about whether or not to acknowledge them. It's simply a question of *how*.

'When I'm putting a ceremony together for someone, I'm reflecting on and commemorating a life that's been lived. I'm validating that person's individuality and helping their family to make a statement about who they were, and what they achieved in life: because if it's just left to history to submit its own report, then the record might not be accurate or complete. So the ceremony is about putting the record straight, because it's the last thing the family can ever do for their loved one.

'Now obviously in Jonathan Flint's case, history is going to record that he was a serial rapist and murderer. But that headline's going to drown out the fact that, whether we like it or not, he was also a loving husband and father; so it's vital that I acknowledge that in the ceremony, because that's how Alex and Tara have the right to remember him. Not to mention it's also the reason we're putting ourselves through all this in the first place.'

'Exactly.' Simon sighed. 'Anyway, what did you make of Alex and Tara?'

'I think Tara's probably in a better place than her sister is. Tara's clearly discharging a lot of the anger she must feel towards her father by rejecting the comfortable middle-class upbringing he gave her and living a more alternative kind of lifestyle.

'Alex on the other hand, I'm not so sure about. She seemed quite cold. And her flat is absolutely immaculate, isn't it? I don't know whether she's got OCD or whether it might be a control thing. I mean, their lives must have absolutely spiralled when their father was arrested, so maybe Alex has a need to assert rigid order in her life now. Of the two of them, I wouldn't be surprised if it's her that might turn out to be the emotional time-bomb.'

'She could do ...' Simon said. 'Although it was Tara that I found awkward to deal with. And not helped by that idiot partner of hers.'

'Yes, I see what you mean about Carl. And you're right: Tara is definitely the more prickly one. But that's what I'm saying:

maybe her putting out all that negative emotion is a healthy thing. We don't know what Alex might be holding in.

'Anyway, we had a good chat and we're all clear about what the funeral needs to be. And as you suggested to them, Alex and Tara want their mother to be included, so the focus of the ceremony is going to be on Jonathan as a husband and father in the times before his wife died.

'Alex and Tara want the curtains to close, because obviously having that sense of an ending is what this is all about for them; and there'll just be one piece of music, which we'll have played in full during a time of reflection. There won't be anything played on entry or exit.'

'What music did you come up with in the end?'

'I'd rather not say just yet. I've chosen a track that's actually something of an 'our tune' for Gill and myself, so I want to run it past her before I commit to using it. It's already on the crem's media system though – I've checked, so we won't have to worry about ordering it. But if Gill's okay with it then I'll run it past Diane Roberts too, just so she knows why it's been chosen. I don't want it causing any offence amongst the crem' staff and I don't want you getting any flack for anything to do with the ceremony. You've got enough to cope with.'

'Thank you.'

'But otherwise I've pretty much got the ceremony sketched out. Alex and Tara don't want to see a preview of the script, which is no bad thing, because that'll give me more time to fine-tune it. And although it's going to be very simple, it's still going to take the best part of twenty minutes to deliver.'

'That's alright,' Simon replied. 'It'll make going to South Wales seem more worthwhile. Did you have to compromise on spiritual content in the end?'

'No, not at all. Like we agreed, I put aside the fact that I'm a humanist and went along with a blank canvas. And after what you'd said about Tara possibly wanting a prayer or two, I actually made a point of leaving some gates open during the conversation; but she didn't wander through any of them. In fact, she didn't raise anything with a spiritual slant at all. So a humanist funeral is what I ended up coming away with after all,' Philip declared.

'Good. That's another dilemma solved. It's all falling into place nicely now then,' Simon replied, genuinely pleased for Philip's sake. 'I've spoken to Marie again and we had a good chat and picked ourselves up and brushed ourselves down.

'She knows why I'm doing the funeral and I explained why we're approaching it the way we are and she's okay with all of that. It's not going to come between us, which is what I was really concerned about.'

'That's really good to know, Simon. I'm pleased about that, although I don't for one minute think you've got anything to blame yourself for anyway,' Philip responded. 'In fact, I was thinking that when this is all over and the dust has settled, that I might catch up with Marie myself, if you don't mind?'

'Course I don't. I think she'd appreciate it. She knows I haven't said anything to you about her reasons for declining, and if she decides to tell you herself, that's up to her. But either way, I think it would be good closure for both of you if you were to have a chat when it's all over.'

'That's what I was thinking. Anyway, back to the here and now: have you got Flint's body yet?'

'We're collecting it tomorrow. Then the proverbial chicken really will come home to roost.'

EIGHT

Simon hadn't felt such anticipation about going to remove a body since the day thirty-two years previously when, as a fifteen-year-old lad on work experience, he'd travelled to Cornwall with his then employer-to-be to collect the body of a man who'd drowned on holiday.

The prospect of visiting a mortuary had been thrilling enough back then, let alone the gruesome frisson of what a drowned body would be like. No different to a normal one as it turned out – the unfortunate victim having been pulled back to the beach by other swimmers who'd attempted to resuscitate him while waiting for an ambulance.

Instead, what had been most vivid was how young the chap had looked. Aged forty-one, he'd been the first premature death that Simon had encountered, having until that point only seen the wizened corpses of the elderly.

Simon also remembered seeing for the first time the brutally ugly line of suturing across the man's trunk where a post-mortem had been performed.

Such things had long ceased to hold any fear or fascination. Mortuaries, post-mortems and bodies immersed in water for far longer than the hapless holidaymaker were now just punctuation marks in Simon's career, and it was only Flint's unique notoriety that was evoking the excitement of his earliest days again now.

The call had come on Wednesday afternoon, while Simon had been putting an order of service sheet together for the printer. Already frustrated with trying to re-format the minister's draft, he'd felt a further stab of irritation when the phone rang and Beverley had said: 'He's sat right here. I'll put you through.'

But his mood had changed when Beverley called out: 'Terry Gregory from the West Mercia Coroner's Office for you.'

'We've had the notification from Mr Armstrong that Jonathan Flint's funeral has been set for Wednesday eleventh of April, at Llancroes Crematorium in South Wales,' Gregory had said.

'Yes, that's right.'

'And I take it you and the crematorium are keeping that a closely guarded secret?'

'Absolutely.'

'Okay, well the coroner is happy to authorise release of Mr Flint's body now. It's being held in the mortuary here at the coroner's court. The release note and the cremation form are already down there for you, so I'll give you the mortuary's number and you can contact them to arrange collection.

'However, once Mr Flint's body is in your care, you'll be responsible for its safety, so I would strongly recommend that you delay collecting it until just before the funeral.'

Simon had been inclined to agree, and indeed Diane Roberts had already granted him some latitude with getting the cremation forms delivered to Llancroes. But it wasn't just a paperwork issue: Tara wanted to view her father's body.

Given the circumstances, Simon knew he would have been quite within his rights to delay removing the body, then put it straight into whatever coffin he had available and say to Tara: 'Right, there he is.' But he would never have dreamt of doing such a thing.

Tara wasn't responsible for her situation, and she had as much right as anyone to see her father's body presented in a proper and sympathetic manner. Indeed, her father's estate was footing the bill for her to do just that.

But it wasn't just about professionalism. Simon felt a genuine desire to make the experience of viewing her father's body a helpful one for Tara. So he'd pretended reluctance when he'd phoned the coroner's mortuary and laying false blame on the crematorium's documents deadline, he'd arranged to remove Flint's body three days before he really needed to.

That was Wednesday morning and so now – Friday afternoon, Simon reached out the driver's side window and pressed the intercom at the rear entrance of the coroner's court. A couple of electronic beeps later there was a tinny-sounding 'Hello?'

Simon leant closer and said loudly: 'Hello. This is Arthur Williams Funeral Directors from Gloucestershire.'

The noise that came back sounded like 'Okay' and the huge wooden gate began rolling aside. Simon drove into the yard within and after manoeuvring in the space between some wheelie bins on one side and a plant machinery cabinet on the other, he reversed the van up to the mortuary doors. As he and David got out of the vehicle they were met by a man in his thirties, dressed in medical scrubs.

'Come to take Mr Flint off our hands then?' the technician said flatly.

'We have indeed,' Simon replied as he opened the tailgate and pulled out a stretcher trolley.

Stepping inside, him and David followed the technician through a vestibule overlooked by a glass screen behind which was the mortuary office and onwards into the body store, where banks of fridge doors filled both sides of the long space.

The numbering on the doors revealed capacity for sixty-five bodies.

Down at the far end another technician – a woman in her forties with spikey red-dyed hair and a roses-and-thorns wrap-round tattoo visible under the sleeve of her scrubs, was hovering expectantly by the much chunkier doors of the deep-freeze section.

Simon felt a stab of alarm. Primarily used for forensic cases requiring retention for further examination, deep freezing of Flint's body would put paid to any chance of viewing by Tara.

But to Simon's immediate relief the woman reached for the handle of the last of the standard fridge doors and swung it open. She waited for her colleague to manoeuvre the scissor-lift trolley into position, then rolled out the lower-most body tray.

Simon felt his pulse quicken at the sight of the white plastic body bag. Of the nearly 6000 bodies he'd seen over the course of his career, none had ever had such an aura of menace and notoriety.

He pulled the elasticated cover off the stretcher and unclicked the straps as the electronic whine of the scissor-lift echoed round the body store. He continued to pretend indifference as the woman technician reached across the bag and undid the L-shaped zip.

Flint's body was dressed in a paper-thin, disposable shroud and his head was wrapped with incontinence pads – a precaution against leakage from the cranial incision after post-mortem.

To Simon's disappointment the technician made no attempt to remove the pads, instead simply tugging back the sleeve of the shroud to expose the plastic wristband. 'Jonathan Edward Flint?'

Simon tilted his head to check. 'Yep, okay. Thank you.'

'No jewellery,' the technician added, holding up the two lifeless hands for Simon's inspection.

'No, okay,' Simon responded again. This wasn't the time to pause and reflect on the horrors those hands had wrought.

The woman zipped the bag up again and together with her colleague hoisted one side of the tray, tilting the body bag towards Simon and David so they could slide it onto the stretcher. Simon fastened the restraining straps and with David's help fitted the elasticated cover back over the body. Behind them the technician rolled the empty tray back into its berth and swung the fridge door shut with a solid, muffled thud.

Her colleague led the way back to the office, where Simon signed the register and took possession of the bright yellow coroner's cremation certificate. Then with David's help he loaded the stretcher back into the van. He shut the tailgate and turned to where the technician was watching from the doorway.

'When's he going?'

'This coming Wednesday,' Simon replied.

'Good luck then.'

'Thank you,' Simon smiled.

'Shall I drive back?' Asked David.

Simon handed him the key. The two of them were now responsible for the most hated man in Britain.

*

If the outbound journey had the quality of an adventure, the homeward run felt more like the getaway from a bank heist.

Simon only had thoughts for their grim cargo and with each passing mile he cast glances at the other drivers around them, wondering what their reactions would be if they knew who – or more accurately *what*, was travelling alongside them.

Simon also monitored the radio, tensing as each news bulletin was due and expecting to hear the words: 'The body of serial killer Jonathan Flint has been released into the hands of undertakers this afternoon.'

Anyone hearing that and seeing a silver Volkswagen Transporter emblazoned with 'Private Ambulance' travelling ahead of them on the motorway would be sure to wonder. And what if one of them just happened to be a journalist keen for a scoop? Or someone with more sinister and vengeful intentions?

Simon's anxiety levels didn't lower by a single degree when he and David arrived back at the funeral home. A well-used public footpath ran adjacent to the yard and Simon cast a wary glance along the wire fence when he got out to open the garage door. When David had reversed inside, Simon took another look around before closing the door again.

They unloaded the stretcher and wheeled it into the mortuary – a large room furnished at one end with a stainless-steel worktop, sinks and a sluice, and filled by a six-body fridge at the other.

Simon unzipped the body bag again and pulled away the incontinence pads so he and David could finally gaze upon the cause of all the trouble.

David peered at the cold-moistened features with the casual indifference that only a retired police officer would have, but for Simon it was as momentous as it was fascinating to be contemplating Flint's lifeless countenance: the sagging jaw and drunken-looking, half-open eyes so characteristic of death seeming in his case to convey a hint of extinguished menace.

But it was definitely him. The swept back, dark brown hair so familiar from all the photos and the police mugshot was now completely grey and cut shorter, but neither death nor years on a prison diet had actually altered Flint's looks very much. He still looked undeniably handsome. And as bodies went, Simon could tell that Flint would actually come up rather well when he'd been got ready for viewing.

Simon didn't enter Flint's details into the mortuary register and on the wipe-clean panel on the fridge door he used Alex and Tara's new surname, writing 'Turner' and the body size – 6'0" x 20'.

In the comments section beneath one internet article that Simon had read about Flint's death, someone had expressed their revulsion at the thought of people's loved ones being kept in the same mortuary as Flint. But with three bodies already stored in the lower tiers of his fridge, consigning Flint to the top left tier was the best that Simon could do to isolate his body from the others. It would be coming out again later that evening anyway.

But as he switched off the lights and shut the mortuary door, the sudden weight of responsibility prompted him to say: 'One of his daughters wants to view, so I've arranged for her to come on Monday evening. But just thinking about it again now, is there any chance you could be around while I do it, just for safety's sake?'

'What time on Monday?'

'Seven o'clock.'

'Yes, I can do that.'

'Thank you, David. I'm sure it'll all go off fine, but ... well, you never know.'

'I think it's a very wise precaution.'

*

By 7.45 pm Simon was back in the yard. He glanced along the footpath again, then unlocked the side door to the annexe and promptly locked himself inside again. Feeling like an intruder in his own property he made his way through to the mortuary, from where the ominous, rhythmic throb of the fridge was pulsing like a heartbeat, giving life to a building dedicated to housing the dead.

He opened the door and reached round for the light switch, superstitiously waiting for the room to flicker into stark, fluorescent illumination before he entered.

It was rare for him to prepare bodies himself nowadays. That was Darren's job. But Simon had decided from the outset that he should be the one to do this and so claim for himself this uniquely intimate place in criminal history. Although, with public feeling towards Flint having been given such feverish and violent-sounding expression, Simon was feeling like an accomplice at what he was about to do.

After getting the body out the fridge again, he unzipped the bag and inspected Flint's face more closely.

It was nothing more than ghoulish curiosity, but who wouldn't have done the same in his position? This was the man who in life had stolen the lives of seven, possibly eight innocent young women and girls and who even in death still had the power to adversely affect Simon's own destiny.

But as he began gathering up the necessary instruments and sundries, he found it grimly amusing to think that not only was he staring straight into the face of evil, he was about to become one of the few people in history to have set its features.

He began by inserting eye caps – thin plastic hemispheres resembling oversized contact lenses – beneath the eyelids. As well as restoring a more natural, rounded appearance to the crumpled, dehydrated eyeballs, they also provided something to press against when he gently stretched the eyelids with his fingertips until they eased enough to remain closed.

It was always a relief to get the eyes closed and with that

lingering sense of Flint's ghostly presence now exorcised, Simon relaxed into his task. The next step was to close the mouth with an oral suture – another task that separated the men from the boys.

Using an aneurism hook to hold the lower lip aside, Simon inserted a curved, surgical needle threaded with ligature cord into the lower gum, running a suture from one side of the jaw to the other. He then hooked back the upper lip and pushed the needle up behind it, bringing it out through the left nostril. After passing the needle through the septum he took it back down through the other nostril and out from behind the upper lip again. With the circular suture completed, Simon cut the cord to leave the ends hanging from the still-open mouth.

Setting the facial features was one of the procedures euphemistically referred to as *care of the deceased*, and unpleasant though it was, the rendering of a person's facial features into a more peaceful and composed appearance was not just for the benefit of relatives wishing to view the body, but also to restore the dignity of the deceased.

But who in their right mind would have wanted to restore the dignity of a serial rapist and murderer? Capping the eyes into which terrified young girls had been forced to stare; and sewing up the mouth that had quietly but firmly uttered the chilling words: *'Do as I say and you'll live without scars. I'm just going to have sex with you.'*

Forcing those thoughts away, Simon held the slackened lower jaw closed with his little finger before tightening and knotting the strands of ligature cord. Then after tucking the strands back into the mouth with a pair of forceps, he tweaked the lightly-closed lips to make them appear natural and relaxed.

He very carefully shaved the face and then combed the hair. It really did look like Flint now. Not that he deserved to. Flint should have been going to the furnace wearing the same slack-jawed expression he'd had from the moment death had sent him down from this world, ready to stand before a higher court.

Relieved that the wet work was finally done, Simon lifted the right arm from where it rested stiffly by the side of the body. He folded the forearm back against the biceps and rotated the folded limb at the shoulder before straightening it out again.

Then, taking hold of the clenched hand, Simon bent it backwards and forwards to loosen the wrist, before hooking his fingers under the curled digits, easing them away from the palm and then squeezing them into a fist again. As he did so, his thoughts strayed back to the first time he'd ever helped prepare a body – that of an elderly woman.

'Take that arm and loosen it up,' his employer had instructed, gesturing to where the right arm and hand were resting stiffly across the hollow of the woman's sunken, green-tinted abdomen.

The forearm had felt cold, clammy and inflexible and it had only yielded to Simon's touch in a very limited, lever-like fashion – as if hinged at the elbow.

'That's rigor mortis,' his employer had explained. 'That's what you've got to loosen.'

'How?' Simon had asked nervously.

'Just flex the joints a bit at a time until the rigor breaks down. She's been dead for over twenty-four hours, so it should be starting to fade again now anyway.'

Simon had diffidently levered the forearm backwards and forwards in tiny motions.

'Be firm with it! You won't break anything,' his employer had said, grabbing the woman's other arm and folding it with frightening firmness before straightening it out again.

'The hand will need loosening too ... like this,' he'd said, yanking the hand backwards and forwards to loosen the wrist, before hooking his fingers under the clenched digits and uncurling them, as if trying to take something from the clutches of a recalcitrant child.

Simon remembered timidly copying his employer's example until he'd felt the clenched, claw-like fingers starting to ease. Already scared he might fracture something, he'd been even more fearful that those lifeless fingers might suddenly grasp his in ghostly reciprocation.

And now, thirty-two years and nearly 6000 bodies later, Simon could feel himself cringing once more as he began manipulating and loosened Flint's fingers, repulsed this time not by the threat of fracture or ghostly response, but simply by the thought of what those hands had done to at least seven helpless, terrified young girls.

With the preparation work finally complete, Simon went through to the workshop and within half an hour he'd fitted and lined a plain oak veneered coffin.

To the average onlooker the finished article might have seemed too elegant a receptacle for someone like Flint. But although Simon could have provided a visibly cheaper-looking coffin, complete with uncoated, brown plastic handles, it would have cost more just to order one in. And anyway, the purposes of everyone involved with the funeral were best served by using a coffin that looked just like any other.

After setting the engraving machine, Simon produced a nameplate with Flint's full name, date of death and age. But instead of fixing it straight onto the coffin lid, he slid it back into its cellophane wrapper and tucked it alongside the box of blanks it had come from. Finished coffin lids were always kept propped against the wall by the mortuary door and Simon didn't want anyone spotting Flint's lid.

He wheeled the coffin into the mortuary, tugged the body bag to the edge of the tray and used it as a sling to lower Flint's body into the coffin. He then tucked the bag down the sides, where it would be covered by the gown and frill.

When Simon had first joined the funeral profession the majority of bodies were dressed in a gown – a taffeta garment with padded lapels and a tasselled cord belt. The gowns came in three sections, all designed so they could be fitted to any size of body with minimal physical effort. Then, to complete the presentation, a matching frill was stapled round the rim of the coffin interior.

Gown sets had only been available in a limited range of colours back then: powder blue; candy pink; plain white; and 'oyster' – a peculiar and sickly colour resembling butterscotch flavoured Angel Delight. But although a much wider and more tastefully-coloured range of gowns was available nowadays, families were opting almost entirely to have their loved ones dressed in their own clothes anyway.

But as he began dressing Flint's body in a plain white gown, Simon noticed how instinctive it still felt to do it: how every fold and tuck of the gown and every click of the staple gun was still just as instinctive as when he'd been doing it every day as a teenaged funeral assistant. In fact, the whole task of preparing Flint's body for viewing no longer felt like the morbid consummation he'd been expecting, but actually something quite routine. And although he was doing it purely for Tara's sake, Simon was acutely aware of how appalled the victims' families would be if they could see the care and attention that he was lavishing on Flint's remains.

With his work finally finished, Simon pumped the scissor-lift back up to height and rolled the coffin into its top-tier berth.

He'd finally informed a stunned Darren that the firm was

handling Flint's funeral, but at least at top-tier height no one else with a reason to be looking inside the fridge – be they staff or doctor – would be able to see who was in the coffin. And with 'Turner' written on the fridge door as well, there was nothing more that could be done to hide Flint's presence.

*

Simon arrived at Llancroes Crematorium just before 9.00 am on Monday morning. Just as he'd hoped, the place was deserted, and as he made his way across the empty car park he carefully surveyed his surroundings.

The crematorium itself was a curious combination of 1950s-era local authority architecture and strangely Mediterranean-looking touches like white-painted walls and arched walkways; but it was reassuring to see that the chapel entrance was well-screened by shrubbery and the filigree blockwork of the porte-cochère. The route that the hearse would have to take seemed clear enough: there'd been a separate little access road signposted 'Cortege Vehicles Only' just inside the gates.

Simon followed the signs for the office.

'Mr Thorley, hello,' Diane Roberts greeted him when he'd been admitted past the reception area.

A woman of larger build, with alert eyebrows, short, wavy hair and dressed in a funeral director-style uniform of short black jacket and pinstripe skirt, Diane didn't look the type to suffer fools gladly – just as Philip Coleridge had indicated.

'Call me Simon, please.'

Diane's rather fierce expression gave way to a kindlier, motherly look as she smiled and for a moment Simon was left wondering if he'd been a good boy or a bad one.

'Right you are, Simon. Very pleased to meet you. Let's get your forms sorted and then I'll show you round.'

Simon handed Diane the cremation forms.

She checked them carefully. 'Pulmonary embolism and retro-peritoneal haemorrhage,' she recited. 'Even murderers have to die of something I suppose,' she added, before handing the documents to one of her administrative assistants.

'It seems strange to see his name on one of our prelim's, isn't it?' The assistant said as she separated out the blue preliminary instructions form and put it in a wire tray containing similar forms.

'It does indeed, Jean,' Diane responded. 'It does indeed …'

'Right, let's show you round then, Simon.' She led him through a side door and into a passageway stacked with stationery supplies and archived files before opening a more ornate wooden door and emerging into the chapel, just behind the lectern.

'I'll be on duty myself for the funeral,' Diane said, as Simon took in his surroundings.

Despite the building's rather dated exterior, the chapel itself was a surprisingly impressive space. The chapels of post-war crematoria often were. Funerals were still exclusively religious affairs in the 1950s and 60s and as a result the interiors of crematorium chapels were designed to resemble those of churches.

Simon gazed up at the arched ceiling that rose high above rows of oak pews around him. There was a stained glass window directly above the catafalque and the chapel was bathed in light from leaded glass windows set high enough in the side walls to guarantee privacy within.

Diane led the way down the burgundy carpeted aisle and unbolted the main doors to reveal a further set of glass outer doors that opened onto the porte-cochère.

'When you come through the main gate take the little road marked 'Cortege Vehicles'. That'll take you round the back of the building and up to y'ere.' Diane gestured with her hand.

'Okay,' Simon nodded.

'Will you be bringing the coffin in a hearse or a closed vehicle?'

'The family want us to use a hearse.'

'That's fine. As long as I know what to look out for,' Diane replied.

'Now, I've 'ad a phone call from South Wales Police,' she continued. 'They've been told about the funeral by Gloucestershire Police.'

Simon felt a stab of anxiety. 'And are South Wales planning to have any officers here?'

'They said they're just going to send an unmarked car to keep an eye on things,' Diane replied, 'unless anything untoward 'appens of course, in which case they'll be ready to send more officers. But like you said, who's really going to suspect that Mr Flint's funeral will be coming all the way down y'ere anyway?'

'Exactly,' Simon agreed. 'But I have to admit, it is quite comforting to know the police will be here to keep an eye on things, all the same.'

'It wouldn't be the first time. We've 'ad other funerals when we've 'ad to 'ave the police y'ere: members of the local criminal fraternity an' that sort of thing. Even a Hells Angel's funeral once. That was an experience, I can tell you …

'Anyway, come back inside and I'll show you where you'll come out.'

Diane showed Simon the exit from the chapel, located at the front close to where they'd first entered from the office. She led him out the exit door as well, showing him the covered walkway that it opened onto, the floral tribute display further on round the corner, and the little layby where the hearse needed to be moved to during the service.

'It's nice and secluded out y'ere, but I'm sure you'll agree that we don't want the family hanging around afterwards. The sooner they're gone again the sooner we can all cover our tracks.'

Simon gave a tight-lipped smile. 'My thoughts entirely. Don't worry – I'll be on to it.'

'Thank you. And you'll be back the following day to collect the ashes?'

'I will. What time will they be ready from?'

'Say ten o'clock to be on the safe side? But I really do want them collected the next day, please.'

'Absolutely. I'll be here at ten o'clock sharp.'

'Good. So we've got a plan then, have we?'

'I think so. You've shown me everything I need to see, thank you. We just need to let it happen now.'

'We do. I'll see you on Wednesday afternoon then. And let's get it done.'

NINE

The funeral home had originally been a Victorian villa. Set back from the road, its substantial gardens had long since been laid to tarmac, with visitors' parking at the front and a driveway to the yard behind. The reception area, arranging lounge and two chapels of rest were on the ground floor and the administration office occupied the first floor. It was from the window by his desk that Simon was keeping watch.

Conducting a viewing on Flint during working hours would never have been an option, but opening up the funeral home out of hours seemed equally rash, and Simon wished he could be doing it under conditions of invisibility. Yet here he was, office lit up and front door unlocked, with the body of Jonathan Flint, serial killer, out on display.

At 6.55 pm a grubby estate car drew to a halt at the end of the drive, then turned in. To Simon's immediate consternation a second car, an altogether newer and cleaner little hatchback, followed. He'd only been expecting Tara and Carl.

It wasn't unknown for hangers-on to turn up for viewings, the family who'd booked the appointment assuming they could invite others to tag along with them, but this most definitely wasn't the occasion for that.

'They're on time at least, but I wasn't expecting anyone other than Tara and her partner,' Simon announced.

'How many of them are there then?' asked David, glancing

up from that week's edition of the local paper spread out in front of him on Beverley's desk.

Simon moved so that he could peer down at his visitors without being spotted himself. To his relief he saw that it was Alex in the second vehicle. 'Oh, it's alright, it's only three of them. The other daughter's obviously decided to come after all.'

He watched impatiently as Alex and Tara lingered outside, chatting and casting wary glances at the building. They would of course be filled with their own anxieties, but Simon wanted them to hurry up and come inside. There was no reason for anyone to know who they were, but he didn't want to test the theory and he decided to go down and open the door to encourage them in. But he'd barely reached the stairwell when he heard the door alert anyway.

Tara was first to enter and Simon immediately saw that she had none of the combative demeanour she'd displayed they'd first met. In fact, she looked decidedly unsure of herself, and Simon's own anxiety quickly gave way to sympathy.

Tara must already have lost so much as a result of her father's crimes and yet the level of public animosity towards him meant she was now at risk of being disenfranchised from the chance even to grieve for him.

Alex on the other hand, seemed as self-possessed and unreadable as before, and Carl just looked impatient.

'Hi,' Simon greeted them all soberly. Once again he got three blank looks in response, so he continued with his usual script for viewings: 'Do you all want to go in together?'

'You two can go in first,' Alex said.

'We've got a lounge if you want to wait in there,' Simon offered.

'I'm fine here, thank you,' Alex responded, immediately perching herself on one of the courtesy chairs by the front door. She wasn't the first to do that.

Simon led the way down the corridor and then paused by the chapel door, his fingers resting on the handle as he turned to face Tara and Carl again. 'He's just dressed in a white gown, but he looks very peaceful and composed.' Once again receiving no reaction, he opened the door and stepped inside.

Like so many visitors before her, Tara faltered at the sight of the coffin – placed with its foot-end towards the wall so she wouldn't immediately be confronted by the sight of her father's face. She cautiously stepped up to the side of the coffin and tilted her head to contemplate what lay within, while Carl made straight for the opposite side, as if to check for himself that Simon had been telling the truth.

Simon had seen it all before and he lingered just long enough to steal a glance at the expressions on their faces and check for tell-tale signs that anything was amiss. At moments like this he was always braced for a sudden exclamation of horror.

After so many years of doing them, he'd grown to dislike conducting viewings because in spite of the many polite 'Thank you's and 'You've made him look so peaceful's, he was equally likely to get a dispiriting: 'It didn't look like Mum/Dad'.

On one occasion he'd even had a very rural-sounding, 'Bugger me ... I wish I 'adn't bloody come now!' to which he'd been tempted to parry back with an equally blunt: 'She's been dead for a week. You can't expect a purse from a sow's ear.' But that wasn't what his visitor had meant and Simon had known it. Even so, if affirmations from grateful clients were trophies, he had long ago resigned himself to knowing that he would sometimes be awarded the wooden spoon.

But right then Tara's face registered nothing except that familiar, tearful look of absorption he'd seen so many times before, and Carl looked predictably unmoved, so Simon withdrew. Conscious that Alex was sitting a few metres behind him he made an extra show of closing the door gently behind him so he could still steal his usual couple of seconds to listen for any comments from within.

He moved back to where Alex was sat, head down and face lit aglow by her smartphone. He wondered if she too was checking the news for anything about her father's funeral. 'You all set for Wednesday?' he asked quietly when she looked up.

'As we'll ever be. Will there be police there, d'you know?'

'According to the crematorium manager, South Wales Police are going to send an unmarked car just to keep a discreet watch on things. But nothing more than that. There won't be a security cordon or anything silly like that.'

The chapel door opened and Tara poked her head out in almost cartoon-like fashion. 'You coming in?'

Alex put her phone back in her bag and went to join her sister, leaving Simon to retreat back upstairs. Then on hearing the three of them emerge from the chapel again ten minutes later he made his way back down again and was surprised to see that even Alex's eyes were reddened with tears.

'Thank you,' she murmured. 'You've done it really nicely.'

'Yeah, he looks really peaceful,' Tara mumbled through tears of her own.

Relieved more than rewarded, Simon responded with a tight-lipped smile. Then into the silence that followed, he said: 'Were the directions clear in the confirmation letter? You know where you're going on Wednesday?'

'Yes, we've looked it up. We've got satnav anyway,' Alex replied.

'I'm sorry it's so far to go. But at least we'll be well out of everyone's way down there, so you should be able to have some peace and privacy.'

'We'd bloody better do,' Carl muttered.

*

Simon had been monitoring the internet throughout the morning and he didn't know whether to be suspicious or relieved that there was no mention of the funeral being due to take place that afternoon.

From the window overlooking the yard he looked down to where Darren was busy washing the firm's Mercedes hearse. Tempting though it was not to bother with cleaning it for the fifty-one-mile journey to Llancroes, a grubby-looking hearse would only have drawn unnecessary attention, particularly as the weather was drying up now anyway.

An hour later Simon went down to the garage to help Darren load the coffin onto the hearse. The presence of Flint's body had been weighing heavily on Simon's mind, and being able to get it off the premises again made the prospect of performing the funeral itself seem strangely less daunting.

It was going to take them about an hour and twenty minutes to get to Llancroes. An hour and twenty minutes travelling with the coffin of the country's most hated man in plain view. But at least when they left the funeral home responsibility for the body would no longer rest solely on Simon's shoulders. If anything happened on the way to the crematorium: if the hearse suffered some kind of mechanical failure, or if by chance someone did realise whose body it was they were transporting, Simon knew he would be fully entitled to call for police assistance.

He picked up the floral tribute he'd ordered on Alex and Tara's behalf and placed it alongside the coffin, sitting it on a pair of friction mats to secure it during transit. Then he closed the tailgate and stood back to take in the sight.

Although the general public would quite rightly have been horrified to see Flint's very respectable-looking coffin in the back of a nice clean, shiny hearse, it was still the simplest and most effective means of ensuring that he could be removed from this mortal realm unnoticed and unacknowledged. After all, what possible reason would anyone have for suspecting that it was him in there? There was nothing to distinguish his hearse and coffin from the hundreds of others that would be arriving at crematoria up and down the country that afternoon.

More considerate drivers might well slow down to let the hearse out of a junction and a pedestrian might even doff their hat (there were still people who did – including, rather reassuringly, the occasional youngster with their baseball cap); and you could always spot the Catholics, because they crossed themselves. But they would only be doing so in response to what they were seeing. They wouldn't know whose coffin it was and Jonathan Flint, the great deceiver, would have struck one last time.

Simon's conscience was perfectly clear at the prospect. Despite Flint's appalling crimes, Alex and Tara still had a right to grieve for the father they'd known and that alone meant the ends would more than justify the means.

Brian – the other bearer Simon had selected to go on the funeral alongside David and Darren, arrived early and full of anticipation. Simon intended to act as the fourth man. Quite apart from wanting to keep the number of staff involved to a minimum, if any press photographers did happen to be there, then it would make the proceedings look so low-key that they hadn't even warranted the presence of a conducting funeral director.

Simon gathered Darren, David and Brian together the office and with Beverley listening in, he delivered his briefing:

'As I said when I booked you all, despite all the official secrecy there's still a risk that there might be press photographers or TV cameras lurking in the crematorium grounds. Consequently we could end up with our pictures on the front page of a newspaper tomorrow morning, not to mention being all over the internet. So firstly thank you all for agreeing to do this funeral.

'Llancroes Crematorium have laid on a four o'clock slot to keep us well away from their other funerals today; but we've also had to book and pay for the two preceding slots as well, just to ensure that there's a buffer zone.'

That elicited a murmur of surprise from Brian, but Simon didn't let it interrupt his flow: 'But if anyone *does* approach you, then the funeral we're doing is that of a Mrs Gloria Turner. The crematorium staff have all been primed to say the same thing. And when we get the hearse out in a minute you'll see that the flowers have been chosen to look suitably feminine as well.

'South Wales Police will be sending an unmarked car to keep an eye on things, but if anything *does* kick off, then I'm sure plenty more officers will be ready to descend on the place.

'And on that subject, I've planned the route with David and if anything untoward does happen on the way there, then we'll just have to let him do whatever needs to be done, safe in the knowledge that we can always change our underwear when we get home. So with that in mind, please make sure your seatbelts are fastened at all times.'

David nodded his agreement.

'Obviously, when we arrive at the crem' I don't want to waste a single second getting the coffin into the chapel and getting the funeral started,' Simon continued. 'But we must still do that in our usual calm and dignified manner. Quite apart from being the best form of camouflage, this is still the funeral of someone's father. So "walk, don't run" is the order of the day.'

'But once we've got the coffin onto the catafalque, we won't bow to it like we normally do. Instead, I just want the three of you to come straight back out and move the hearse round by the chapel exit, where it'll be more out of sight; then stay there with it. And at the end of the service just come back in through the exit door to get the flowers straight off the coffin, like you do at Lewiston.

'And one last point, but it's the most important one: fifty percent of this exercise is about getting Jonathan Flint cremated safely and discreetly. But the other fifty percent is about his daughters finally being able to get some closure after ten years of living under the shadow of their father's crimes.

'They never had the faintest idea what he'd been up to until he was arrested and so for them, today is about saying goodbye to the man they only ever knew as a loving father – not the man the rest of us have come to know as a serial murderer.'

That elicited a couple of sombre looks and pensive murmurings, before Simon added: 'Any questions?'

'That was an excellent briefing. Well done,' said David.

'Yeah, that's put it in a totally different light. I hadn't ever thought about it like that,' Brian added. 'So who's actually taking the service then?'

'Good point,' Simon replied. 'Philip Coleridge is doing it. So obviously it's going to be a humanist ceremony.'

Philip had remained uncharacteristically reticent about the ceremony and Simon still didn't know what it would actually consist of. He didn't even know what the music was going to be. But this funeral was always going to be as unique a challenge for Philip as it was for him, and Simon respected the fact that Philip would need every last minute there was to prepare himself and his script.

'Right, last call for the toilets and then we'd better get going,' Simon announced.

He turned to Beverley as the others dispersed. He felt guilty at leaving her to lock up the funeral home on her own; but they weren't due at Llancroes until 4.00 pm and Beverley would be gone well before news of the funeral would have a chance to break. 'I'll see you tomorrow then – all being well.'

'Good luck,' Beverley replied. 'I hope I don't see you all on the Six O'Clock News!'

'Don't even think it ... And you'll take the phones on your mobile?'

'Yes. I'm still happy to keep them overnight if you want some peace and quiet when you get back.'

'No, it's fine, thank you. I'll take them when I'm back. I don't want you having to fend off any unwanted calls if word *does* get out.'

Simon went down to the yard to join the others. David was busy making final adjustments to the driver's seat and door mirrors and in the rear Darren and Brian were fastening their seatbelts.

This was it. Three long weeks since that fateful phone call from Colin Armstrong and now it was time to put all the plans into action. It was easy to forget that this was really just a long trip out, a quickie private committal and then home again.

They coasted gracefully through the town just as they had countless times before, but Simon couldn't help but feel a twinge of guilt as people cast respectful glances and a van driver stopped to allow them through at the usual pinch point by the shops. But finally they got out onto the main road and into the safety of relative anonymity.

The weather had cleared up after a damp and cloudy morning and generous amounts of blue sky were now appearing through the clouds. Simon sat in silence, while David concentrated on driving. But in the back of the hearse Darren and Brian attempted the usual chit-chat until they too lapsed into silence. They left Bybrook behind them and after six miles of open road they finally reached the junction with the M5.

As David increased speed on the slip road, Simon felt his anxiety levels rising at a similarly rapid rate. To see a fully-laden hearse on the motorway wasn't exactly unheard of, but it was still unusual enough that they would be sure to attract a certain amount of attention and Simon had to remind himself that they had all the camouflage they needed.

David had the hearse at a steady 70 mph in lane one, but that soon felt like a stately pace as other traffic began overtaking them. Simon cast glances at the occupants of each passing vehicle, half expecting to see someone mouth the words 'I wonder if that's Jonathan Flint in that hearse'. But apart from idly curious looks, they didn't seem to be attracting any unwarranted attention.

Stopping to pay the toll on the Severn Bridge felt like a Carry On film moment, but even that passed uneventfully – the other motorists around them more concerned with getting through the pay booths themselves than with the fact that there was a hearse at the next booth along.

Once they were into Wales Simon heard his phone ringing in his coat pocket and immediately tensed when he saw 'Philip Coleridge mobile' on the screen.

Philip had opted to make his own way to Llancroes, wanting to be there in good time to check in with Diane Roberts and get himself settled and prepared. He'd also agreed to meet Alex, Tara and Carl upon their arrival and lead them straight into the chapel, out of sight.

'Hi, Philip,' Simon said, his heart starting to thump.

'Hi, Simon. Just phoning to say that I've arrived and that everything looks fine so far. The two-thirty is only a committal, so there's going to be plenty of blank space before ours. Alex and Tara aren't here yet, but there's no sign of any press reporters or TV cameras and no one seems to be loitering with intent.'

'Brilliant. That's good to know. Thank you. We're over the bridge and on schedule, so we'll see you in a bit.'

When the signs for their motorway exit finally came into view, Simon took out his phone again and switched it to silent while he remembered. He kept the phone in his hand then, knowing he wouldn't feel it vibrating in his coat pocket. Sure enough, minutes later he felt his phone throbbing in his hand. It was Philip again.

'Hi, Philip. All okay?'

'Yes. I'm just calling to say that Alex, Tara and Carl are here now and that we've taken them straight into the chapel. Two police officers have also turned up and they're going to keep watch at the front and rear of the building. But other than that, the coast is still clear at the moment.'

When he'd finished the call, Simon twisted round in his seat. 'Philip Coleridge has given us the all-clear, but just in case there are any photographers hiding in the bushes when we arrive, remember to act natural.'

'In other words, if we *do* see any photographers or TV cameras in plain sight, then don't stare straight ahead and ignore them, because that *will* look suspicious,' David pitched in. 'Remember, this isn't Jonathan Flint we've got in the back – it's Mrs Gloria Turner; so look as if you're wondering why on earth there are TV cameras or press photographers there.'

Grateful for that bit of advice, Simon felt his heart rate quickening again as they joined the road where the crematorium was situated. Then, just as the chimney and then also the chapel roof came into view, his phone began vibrating and yet again 'Philip Coleridge mobile' was showing on the screen.

Simon felt torn. If there *were* cameras waiting for them, he didn't want to be captured on film using his phone in the hearse. But whatever Philip wanted now, it had to be important.

'Where are you now?' Philip said, the moment Simon answered.

'Just approaching the crematorium gates. What's up?'

'We've got some spectators. Sounds like they've picked something up on Carl's Facebook page.'

'Oh, for fuck's sake... Shit! Well ... it's too late now, we'll just have to brazen it out,' Simon said loudly, to alert the others. He glanced at David as he spoke and was reassured to notice a subtle, but instant alteration in David's demeanour.

'How many of them are there?'

'Just two of them. A young couple. Diane and the police are speaking to them now.'

'Alright, we're just coming through the gates now. I'll have to go,' Simon snapped. He ended the call and gestured for David to follow the 'Cortege Vehicles Only' sign.

'Okay chaps, sounds like we've got a couple of spectators after all,' Simon announced. 'Philip thinks they've picked up something on Facebook. Anyway, the police are onto them, so hopefully we'll be okay. Just act natural, but keep your faces turned away if you do see anyone pointing a mobile phone at us.'

They followed the access road round the back of the crematorium and as they came up the other side and approached the port-cochère, Simon glanced across to the car park. Sure enough there were two plain clothes police officers, recognisable only by their black utility vests, stood talking to a young couple. A steely-faced Diane Roberts was marching back down the path while Philip, in his customary dark grey suit and navy blue tie, was waiting by the chapel doors.

Simon felt a stab of regret at having put Diane in this position. There was always a risk that news of the funeral would break in time for someone to turn up and watch, but he'd never for one minute imagined that it would end up being an inside job.

Seething with frustration and anxiety, as soon as the hearse drew to a halt he got out and greeted Diane with: 'Has our cover been blown?'

'No, not really. They're friends of one of the daughters' partner – Carl is it? They picked up on something he put on Facebook last night and they thought they'd come down y'ere to watch,' Diane replied. 'They're just ghouls, that's all.'

'That's bad enough,' Simon sighed, shaking his head. 'I flaming well despair. I really do.'

'Nothing we can do about it now,' Diane said calmly. 'The police are dealing with it.' She turned to where Darren, Brian and David had taken their places at the rear of the hearse, steadfastly ignoring what was going on around them. 'Can I just check the nameplate please, gentlemen,' she said, stepping between them.

'Clever touch with the flowers, Simon,' she added, nodding at the floral MUM sat alongside the coffin. 'Is that just for show, or do you want me to carry it in for you?'

'No, there is a reason for having it, so if you could carry it in that would be really helpful. Thank you.' And with Darren's help, he gingerly extracted the frame.

'Let's get on with it then. The family are in there ready,' Diane said once she'd taken hold of the MUM. Philip had already gone inside to take his place at the lectern.

Simon shot another glance at the young couple – ironically now stood watching alongside the two police officers – and wondered if they'd been able to capture anything on their phones before the police had intervened. It was too late now anyway: there was nothing more he could do about it. And meanwhile he still had a funeral to perform.

The four of them pulled the coffin out of the hearse, turned it through ninety degrees and then hoisted it onto their shoulders. Darren and David were at the rear – the head end, with Simon and Brian leading at the foot. Simon waited a few seconds until he could feel that everyone had the weight settled on their shoulders, then said quietly: 'Okay chaps.'

They stepped off in unison, with Diane bringing up the rear. Once they got inside the chapel Simon felt himself relaxing ever so slightly, but from where he was carrying at front left, the coffin blocked his view of Alex, Tara and Carl.

On reaching the catafalque the four of them slid the coffin off their shoulders again and placed it onto the rollers. As Simon had instructed, they dispensed with the customary bow and instead remained motionless as Diane placed the MUM on the catafalque. As she did so, Simon stole a sideways glance at Alex, Tara and Carl before leading the bearers back down the aisle.

Darren, Brian and David duly headed back outside and Simon couldn't help but feel sorry for them. The advent of on-site cafes and hospitality suites at two of their local crematoria meant the bearers could now look forward to a cup of coffee while they waited around during funerals. But after the long journey down to Llancroes, their only reward today would be to get to use the toilets.

Simon was already feeling a sense of accomplishment though, and as he took station at the back of the chapel alongside Diane, he knew his duties were now largely discharged. Staring back up the aisle, he took great satisfaction in reciting to himself the opening paragraph of the cremation regulations:

> 'The Funeral Director is responsible for the provision of sufficient bearers to convey the coffin from the hearse to the catafalque. When the coffin is in position on the catafalque or deposited in the rest room or Chapel of Rest at the Crematorium, the responsibility of the Funeral Director towards it ceases and that of the Cremation Authority begins.'

Carl craned his head round – a behaviour that Simon always found irritating at funerals. Why couldn't people just concentrate on what they were there for, instead of looking round to see what else might be going on?

If Carl was hoping to catch him easing the boredom by sharing a quiet joke with Diane or looking at his phone – which admittedly a few too many of his fellow funeral directors were guilty of – then he was going to be disappointed. Instead, Simon set the example by standing to attention and focusing his attention solely on Philip.

This was no time for distractions. Having been responsible for orchestrating this most controversial and secretive of events, and having had final custody of the now-historic character at its centre, the moment had come to hear what Philip had found to say to deliver Alex and Tara from their tragic past and the legacy of their father's crimes.

TEN

With his half-moon glasses perched on the end of his nose, Philip cut an almost headmasterly figure as he gripped the sides of the lectern and regarded his tiny congregation with a solemn gaze. He shifted his weight onto his left foot and made a show of drawing breath, as if deciding what to say; but Simon knew full well that every word Philip was about to utter would have been carefully scripted, edited and agonised over until probably well into the previous night.

'Welcome. Our normal routines have been set aside this afternoon for an occasion that was only ever destined to be challenging and demanding.

'Normally for someone's funeral we would gather openly and pay tribute to their life, their achievements and the positive impact they made on all the people they came into contact with while they were alive. Even their wrongdoings, if significant enough to be mentioned, would probably be treated with indulgence and perhaps even humour.

'But today we are gathered in a very different way and for a very different reason. We have gathered quietly, unobtrusively and without any pretence that things are any different than they actually are. We have gathered in the knowledge that you – Alex and Tara – both recognise and acknowledge only too well how one person's actions can have such profound and far-reaching effects on the lives of others: effects so serious that there can never be any prospect of healing.

'With that in mind, you have both asked that we acknowledge that fact today by remembering the young women and girls whose lives your father so cruelly took. It wouldn't be appropriate or respectful to speak their names during this ceremony, but we know who they are. So let us all stand for a few moments of silence in honour of their memories.'

As Alex, Tara and Carl rose to their feet, Simon tilted his head forwards and closed his eyes, fixing in his mind's eye the names and faces of the young women and girls he'd become so familiar with from their photographs in the media and on the internet. Grateful for this unexpected chance to pay his own respects to the victims, he tried to imagine as vividly as he could the sheer, blind terror that each of them had suffered at Flint's hands. He felt he owed them that much at least.

Aleksandra Mazurek ... Lauren Harper ... Sharon Patwell ... Katie Ritton ... Lucy Heaton ... Leanne McDonald ... Ellie Garrett ... and possibly Emma Simms ...

'Thank you,' Philip said, gesturing for Alex, Tara and Carl to sit down again.

'So then, we are not here to celebrate or commemorate your father's life. And yet, the fact that you are here at all is testament to just how strong the familial ties that bind us really are; no matter how strained they might become on life's journey – or even when they break completely, with no apparent hope of being repaired.

And neither is this the time to be looking for answers that we might never find. We are gathered here in the shadow of the unanswerable; the unthinkable; the unimaginable. But we cannot use this short time to dwell on all that has passed. Others in the proper positions of authority have already done that and they have delivered their verdict according to the laws of this country. Meanwhile countless others – most with no personal connection whatsoever – have said their own piece vigorously and publicly, either through the media or through online social networks.

'No, we are here simply in the hope that this simple ceremony will bring a much needed sense of closure for you, Alex and Tara, and that it might enable you both to find a sense of new beginnings as you look towards the rest of your lives.'

Time felt as if it had come to a standstill; and as Simon absorbed Philip's words, he knew they were as necessary for him – and quite possibly Diane – to hear, as they were for Alex and Tara themselves: that by its very nature this ceremony would be the key to enabling all six of them present in the chapel at that moment to reconcile themselves with their individual reasons for being there.

Alex and Tara – and presumably even Carl to some extent, although it was hard to imagine it having the impact on him that it should have done – had been living under the shadow of Flint's crimes for eleven years. But before they could grieve for the man they had only ever known as their father, or resolve their unfinished grieving for their mother, they first needed absolution from their father's crimes.

Diane had, 'on humanitarian grounds' as she'd put it, generously made available the facilities at Llancroes; and Philip had accepted the challenge of delivering the ceremony and of finding a way to express the inexpressible. And for his own part, Simon had accepted the responsibility of orchestrating this whole event, knowing there might well be a price to be paid for his altruism.

That price had just risen significantly thanks to the intrusion of Carl's friends; and although there was no way of knowing what the consequences would be, at least the police had been on hand right from the outset and hopefully they'd managed to prevent the couple from capturing anything useable on their phones.

But it was out of his hands now; and having got this far, all that mattered for the next twenty minutes or so was what was unfolding right there in front of him.

'At your request, our time here today will be spent without reference or recourse to religion. It wasn't something that ever featured in your father's life in a significant way, and of all the complications he might have encountered – and most certainly caused – during his span of years, religion is one element that does not now need to be included at the end of it.

'But your father did once have a greater meaning to his life. He started life as a son and a brother. He grew to become a young man making his own way in the world; and he later fell in love and became a husband and a father – an integral part of a new family unit.

'You tell me he took those responsibilities very seriously and exercised them with great love, and that you both retain very happy memories of those times.

'But somewhere down the line something changed for your father, and however much we may try to pin-point how or when that change began, it will inevitably and inexorably lead us to ask that most important but impossible question: "Why?"

'We all learn from the good example of those who have gone before us on clear and level paths; and equally we can learn a great deal from the experiences of those whose paths have been more winding and rocky. But we also have to come to terms with the wanderings of those who have become lost, sometimes of their own free will, down in the trackless valleys where quicksand and ravines await.

'We have to come to terms with it because, whether by

association or genetic inheritance, we are bound to *all* those who have gone before us; and by that same definition we in turn will continue to be an influence to those who will follow us.

'The innocent and the guilty stare back at us from the far reaches of time and we cannot deny their existence, however much we may want to erase them from history.

'Because of that, we might sometimes feel that we are destined to live under perpetual shadow; that the darkness will never give way to a new dawn. But that shadow is only there to remind us that we must never lose sight of those whose lives have been irrevocably affected either by our own actions or by those of other human beings. Those who, through no fault of their own, have become enveloped by circumstance and fate.

'The two of you must feel similarly enveloped by circumstance, and that fate has set out to deal you the cruellest set of cards that it could.

'You might well have given in to thinking that life is hugely unfair and unjust. But as human beings we all possess within ourselves the courage and the strength to overcome many harsh and uncompromising predicaments, even if sometimes we can only do so with the support of others who are willing to stand patiently and steadfastly at our side.

'So may I venture to suggest that nothing is ever beyond anyone's grasp, and that in spite of the storm clouds which have gathered over your lives during the last eleven years, and which may yet continue to linger, the opportunity to move forward into the sunlight still remains – no matter how improbable that prospect might seem right now.

'Life should be lived fully and experienced deeply, free from doubt or regrets. And so despite whatever may lie in store for you in the future, your personal destinies still lie in your own hands; moulded in no small part by the loving foundation that you have both spoken about so fondly from your childhoods, and by the positive qualities that were undoubtedly imparted to you by your parents during that time.

'You have told me that before the darkness of more recent times descended, you had always felt that you were born from love and into love, and that you have both inherited your mother's kindness, tolerance and humanity.

'You have also told me about the positive character traits that your father displayed when you were younger: his ability with practical things like adjusting your bicycles when you were learning to ride; his sense of humour and his ability to impersonate television celebrities; the patient way he would help you with your maths homework; and even how he would grudgingly surrender the TV remote control to your mother and sacrifice the chance to watch the football.

'There is no doubt that your father felt the loss of your mother as deeply as you both did; and as you saw for yourselves at the time, the large attendance at her funeral was testament to just how much your mother meant to so many other people as well.

'But after she died, your father had to summon all the strength he had to hold things together for you, his daughters: particularly as you, having barely begun your own lives, had already lost such an important guiding light.

'And given the incomprehensible events that were to follow, it is perhaps reasonable to ask whether your father lost *his* guiding light as well.

'That is not to imply that your mother's death was in any way whatsoever to blame for what was to follow, but simply to acknowledge that grief is a deeply powerful emotion and that it can sometimes provoke wildly unpredictable effects.

'We might never know the reasons for your father's crimes,

and it is not your responsibility as his daughters to seek the reasons, or to provide any explanation. And in recognition of that, this ceremony is not just about drawing a line under those things, but also about remembering that there were other, more positive and life-affirming times that came before.

'With that in mind, we will shortly listen to a piece of music. The question of whether to include music today was always going to be a delicate one; but in the end you asked me to choose something suitable to accompany a time of reflection.

'And "reflection" is very much the right word, because we are not in any way seeking to lighten the mood or distract ourselves from our true purpose for being here. We are simply looking to provide you with a means by which to recall happier times with *both* your parents, and possibly even encourage thoughts of those better times which must surely be yet to come.

'With that in mind, I've chosen a song which I think conveys precisely the right kind of sentiment for today, even though it's probably a long way from being the sort of music the two of you might normally choose to listen to. It's not a song that has any direct significance to your father; and it's certainly not one that he ever expressed a wish to have played at his funeral. And neither for that matter is it a song that held any significance for your mother.

'What prompted me to choose it was simply hearing you talk about your memories of your parents; memories that could so easily have been erased by the darkness that followed.

'It's very easy to become overly sentimental at funerals. But I firmly believe that in your particular circumstances, and on this day of all days, you more than anyone have every right to cast a poignant and nostalgic look over your shoulders at how you once were as a family.

'In nineteen seventy-three a film based around that very

theme was released. "The Way We Were" went on to become a cinema classic and its theme song became a huge success in its own right. It's that song which I've chosen for today.

'So as we listen to it, let the words take you back to better, happier times and remind yourselves once more of the love that your parents had for each other, and the love they undeniably had for the both of you.'

From her place at Simon's side, Diane stepped back into the alcove where the organ stood silent and closed up for the day.

Llancroes was equipped with the same media system as Lewiston, and from the corner of his eye Simon could see Diane looking at a computer screen and operating the mouse next to it. She clicked on a green square marked 'Play' and within seconds a familiar piano tune starting playing and Barbra Streisand's unmistakeable humming introduction to "The Way We Were" began to echo around the chapel.

Just as secular, celebration-of-life ceremonies were increasingly taking the place of religious funerals, so recorded music was increasingly taking the place of traditional hymns that people no longer knew, let alone had the slightest inclination to try singing.

Simon's own relationship with hymn-singing had started at school, and what excellent training those countless morning assemblies had eventually turned out to be. He had never suffered the slightest embarrassment at joining in with the singing at funerals and indeed he quite enjoyed helping to belt out tub-thumping old standards like 'How Great Thou Art' and 'Guide Me, O, Thou Great Redeemer'.

But while a generation of crematorium organists was being relegated to operating CD players and media systems, certain pieces of contemporary music they were now expected to DJ for were already becoming as hackneyed as the hymns they had replaced.

The joke around 'Smoke Gets In Your Eyes' by The Platters and 'Always Look On The Bright Side Of Life' by Monty Python had worn so thin that it was almost embarrassing; and groups like Westlife and Queen and contemporary classical singers like Katherine Jenkins, Sarah Brightman and Andrea Bocelli were all now enjoying Las Vegas-style residencies at crematoria up and down the country.

But this was no time for cheap cynicism and Simon silently congratulated Philip on his clever, if somewhat left-field choice. Playing any kind of song would have been courageous on a day like this, and schmaltzy though 'The Way We Were' undoubtedly was, there really wasn't anything more appropriate.

It was also quite amusing, because from what Simon knew of the film, he could just imagine Philip and his wife going to see it as a young couple. As a pair of floppy-haired and flared university types it would have been right up their street.

The violin accompaniment swooped in and Simon felt his eyes prickling with tears. He tried to blink them away, not daring to imagine what Diane would think if she were to see him wiping his eyes. But the sense of poignancy was almost palpable, and it prompted Simon to imagine what it must have been like for Alex and Tara to have what should have been the happiest and most carefree time of their lives stolen from them, firstly by the loss of their mother and then by the horrors that were to follow.

He saw Alex turn her head slightly and glance at her sister, but Tara remained motionless, staring straight ahead. Simon wondered if she too was lost in tearful contemplation, or whether she was simply waiting for it all to end.

Carl was fidgeting next to her and if it was because he didn't want to be there, then it was a sentiment that Simon wholeheartedly shared. What was unfolding there in the chapel was really too profound for the presence of an ignorant oaf like Carl to be tolerated.

The song moved up-tempo with a very 1970s-sounding rhythm, and for a brief moment Simon wondered if it was such a good choice after all. All else aside, this was still the funeral of a man who'd been responsible for the sickening and brutal deaths of at least seven young women.

But the tempo slowed down again, and as the song returned to its more wistful and plaintive beginnings, Simon's thoughts once more returned to what was unfolding right then.

He hoped with all his heart that his and Philip's efforts would be enough: that with Diane's generous cooperation they might genuinely have succeeded in creating a moment in which Alex and Tara could finally lay their both parents to rest and find release from the shadow of their father's crimes.

All too soon the music ended and after a few moments of silence Philip stepped forwards once more.

'And so what of your father now?

'As we speak, numerous editorials and sensationalist headlines are surely already being written, and post-script chapters will soon be added to books that have already been published. But I'm sure all of that is irrelevant to you now.

'Your father is not here to give an account of himself and we cannot assume or speculate what might otherwise have happened in his later years. What we can say though, is that now his life is over, yours can begin afresh. Not in quite such literal terms perhaps, but at least in a new and more positive direction, free from the shackles that have held you back till now.

'We need to remind ourselves that death is not the victor here. It is the continuing and whole-hearted affirmation of life which will have the final say.

'It is only the unloved who go unmourned, and when you leave here to continue with your lives, you will do so carrying precious memories not only of your mother, but also of your father as you both knew him – and not as other people have come to know him. And although the events and actions which have come to define your father in that way must always continue to be regarded with deep regret and sober reflection, they belong now to the past, not the future.

'Marcus Aurelius, a Roman Emperor of the second century AD wrote: "A little while and you will be nobody and nowhere, nor will anything you now behold exist; nor one of those who are now alive. Nature's law is that all things change and turn and pass away, so that in due order different things may come to be."

'It would be very easy for someone in my position to claim that "time is a great healer" and to repeat any number of other well-meaning and – in this situation especially – meaningless clichés. I know that you are still mourning the loss of your beloved mother, and no one has the formula as to the right way to grieve, or for how long.

'But while the actions and events that were to dominate the later part your father's life overtook and overthrew everything which befell your mother, that does not mean that the influence she had upon your lives, nor indeed all the things she achieved in her life, are in any way diminished. Indeed, I am absolutely certain that history will look kindly upon her, as it will upon the both of you.

'In a short while, we will commit your father's body to the flames. I hesitate to use the term "bid him farewell" because you have already expressed understandably ambivalent feelings about the significance of this moment.

'But you have also made the point that he was, and will always be, your father – the man who gave you both life. And so, before the curtains close, some words by another ancient character: the playwright William Shakespeare, who was famed for his astute observations about his fellow man: 'The evil that men do lives after them; The good is oft interred with their bones."

Philip discreetly pressed the button on the lectern and a pair of voile curtains began closing in slow-moving unison across the coffin. Then, as they met in the middle, a pair of burgundy velvet curtains followed and the lighting above the coffin began to dim. The coffin and the floral MUM faded from sight behind the voile and then that too disappeared as the velvet curtains closed.

Simon had never seen a two-stage curtain like that and he was struck by how it softened the stark finality of the moment.

It was different with burials, because there was always that opportunity to take a last look into the grave before walking away. But cremation offered no such simplicity and reassurance. The ubiquitous curtain not only brought a sense of artificiality to the proceedings, but also did nothing to remove those lingering doubts as to what actually happened to the coffin afterwards. And even when a family requested that the curtain remain open, there was the psychological untidiness of walking away from the deceased, rather than properly seeing them off.

Jonathan Flint had left behind more psychological untidiness than any human being ever had a right to, and it was only right that he should be seen to be clearly and unequivocally dispatched. And now that he was, Simon's responsibilities were all but at an end. He still had to make one final and altogether more anonymous return to the crematorium the following morning to collect the ashes, but that would be a simple task in comparison.

In the meantime, all that remained now was to make a discreet exit when the ceremony was over; and in hope of that happening, Simon silently offered up his favourite line from the "Nunc dimittis": "*Lord, now lettest thou thy servant depart in peace according to thy word.*"

Philip turned to face his tiny congregation again. 'And so, we must now look to the future, whatever it might hold. Your father has left a great deal of suffering, strife and notoriety in his wake and while in these final moments of a funeral ceremony we would usually make a concluding reference to a person's legacies, it is not appropriate to do that today.

'He was your father and he was your mother's husband – with all the intricate strands that those relationships entail. But beyond that we cannot afford him any further honour. It is entirely possible that he himself would not have wished to be remembered in any meaningful way, and indeed the very public and tragic consequences of his criminal actions have already denied him that right.

'There were people whose lives your father influenced for the better; but there were many others whose lives he affected for the worse, if not destroying them completely. And there can be no reconciliation between the two.

'But we must turn our focus now onto those who matter most: on you – Alex and Tara; and on those who will have to continue living with the suffering brought about by your father's crimes. And we must also maintain a focus upon the memory of your mother, who has continued to be a constant source of comfort to you in a world of turmoil, even after her own death.

'So let us return to our own lives then, knowing that your family ties – which of course can never be reversed, have led you through some truly dark and appalling times. But hopefully you can now move forwards into a future in which you will be able to throw off the shackles of a bleak past – a past for which you were never responsible anyway.

'After all that has happened, I believe it is the very least you deserve.'

ELEVEN

Philip removed his glasses and stepped away from the lectern. But instead of moving to stand in front of the curtains and give his customary bow, he turned towards the exit. Diane made her way up the aisle with commendably unhurried paces and unlocked the door, and while Philip proceeded out to the covered walkway, Diane remained where she was, respectfully holding station with her hands crossed in front of her and her eyes fixed on the middle distance.

It was over. The footnote to the case of Jonathan Flint, serial killer, had been written and another dark chapter of British criminal history was now complete.

Simon had a vivid image in his mind of standing in the 'True Crime' section of a bookshop at some future point, reading about this very moment:

'Flint, who was convicted of killing seven young women, died in hospital on 7 March 2018, aged fifty-two years, having served just ten years of a life sentence. He was cremated at Llancroes Crematorium, South Wales, on 11 April 2018 in a service attended only by his two daughters. A number of crematoria in and around Flint's home county of Gloucestershire had previously refused to accept his body.'

Wonderful though it would be for that to remain the sum total of public knowledge about the funeral, the intrusion by Carl's friends meant that news headlines screaming: 'Classic movie theme played at serial killer's funeral' was now a depressingly distinct possibility. And rather than a moment of quiet triumph in a corner of a bookshop, Simon knew he might instead be faced with having to read excruciatingly misleading accounts of the funeral, complete with a photo of him and the bearers.

No proper context for the references to Flint as a loving husband and father and the playing of 'The Way We Were' could ever be provided by someone who hadn't been involved with arranging the funeral or been there at its unfolding.

If anything, this had been a courageous event. One in which Alex and Tara had not only been given the chance to free themselves of the past, but also the encouragement to take the first steps towards a new and better future.

Simon began making his way up the aisle with slow, deliberate paces of his own, reluctant even in this instance to make Alex and Tara feel rushed. Whatever might be awaiting them beyond the relative sanctuary of the crematorium and its grounds, and whatever consequences he might personally have to face as the funeral director responsible, he'd managed to deliver Alex and Tara this far and there was no reason to rush them in these final, delicate moments. A funeral was essential treatment against the mental and emotional distress that followed a bereavement, and you couldn't just tip the patient out of bed the moment you'd given them their medication.

And anyway, Philip's words had been genuinely moving to listen to, and in comparison to the flustered state in which he'd arrived barely half an hour earlier, Simon now felt almost anaesthetised. He hoped with all his heart that Alex and Tara had found the ceremony equally as cathartic.

But Alex, dressed in a black trouser suit, was quick to her feet and she stepped out of the pew and made for the exit door without so much as a backward glance at her sister. Carl also stood up, but still Tara remained resolutely motionless.

Recalling how unsure of herself she'd looked when she'd arrived for the viewing, and seeing her sat there now, Simon felt another swell of compassion and he felt completely at one with her reluctance to leave the insulating quietness of the chapel.

And why *should* she be rushed? Having got this far, Tara probably just wanted a few more moments of contemplation before getting up to face the world again, and no one was more entitled to that than her.

She'd arrived in a state of anonymity that she'd never chosen for herself; a state of pseudo-being that had been thrust upon her by well-meaning officialdom. And now, after eleven years of living under the shadow of her father's crimes, she had finally been able to witness them – and him – being consigned to the past.

How cruel then, to steal these last few moments of peace and privacy from her, particularly as she might soon have to face the prospect of her true identity being exposed across the internet and on social media. Simon felt a strong sense of solidarity with her, knowing that he too was facing a similar risk of exposure.

The answer to *that* question lay with the two police officers hopefully still keeping watch outside; and despite his every instinct being towards patience with Tara at that moment, he was eager to catch up with the officers before they left, simply to find out if Carl's friends had managed to succeed in capturing anything on their phones.

Simon tried not to watch as Carl hovered impatiently over Tara before finally stepping over her feet and getting out of the pew. He still had his scuffed boots on, but this time he'd teamed his faded jeans with a corduroy jacket.

Carl marched straight out to the covered walkway, where Simon could see Alex and Philip lingering silently and apart. Carl shouldered his way between them and headed further on down the walkway before stopping and reaching into his pockets. Within moments he was cupping his hands around a cigarette and lighting it.

Simon wondered if he was actually aware that a couple of his friends had travelled down to witness the funeral. But as he continued to steal glances at Carl puffing away on his cigarette, Simon saw the hearse in the background – and that it wasn't just David, Darren and Brian standing alongside it, but one of the police officers too.

Simon felt an immediate surge of relief. If he wasn't able to speak to the officer himself, he knew he could rely on David to establish precisely what had happened with Carl's friends.

But as it was, the police officer looked reassuringly relaxed and although he was clearly still keeping watch, he was doing so with his hands tucked back into the arm-holes of his utility vest. Simon took that to be a good sign.

Meanwhile, Tara was getting to her feet. Dressed in a black leather biker jacket and black jeans, she side-stepped her way out of the pew and approached the curtains. 'Bye, Dad,' she said in an almost child-like voice, before turning to face Simon. 'What happens to the flowers?'

'They'll be brought out in just a moment,' Simon replied. From the corner of his eye he could see Darren and David waiting to come back in and retrieve them. He also knew that in the transfer room behind the chapel a cremator technician would be waiting to open the hatch and pull the coffin through the moment he got the signal that the chapel was clear. And rightly so. The sooner Flint's body was committed to the flames now, the better.

Simon followed Tara out and left Diane to let Darren and Brian slip back in before closing the door again.

Simon stood next to Philip and assumed a similar air of polite abeyance as Tara and Alex stood apart from each other, both clearly lost in their own thoughts. Carl lingered further on down the walkway, wreathed in a haze of cigarette smoke, and across by the hearse David and the police officer stood gazing back at this silent tableau.

Alex was the first to speak: 'You'll collect the ashes, won't you? We don't have to wait for them now, do we?'

'No, no. I'm coming back again tomorrow morning to collect them,' Simon replied. 'You sure you don't want me to bring them over to Cheltenham for you?'

'No, I finish work early on a Friday so I was thinking we could we come and pick them up from your office then, if that's alright.' Alex replied. She glanced at Tara. 'You're still going to come with me, aren't you?'

'I said I would, didn't I?' came the response.

'It'll be four-thirty, four forty-five-ish by the time we get to you,' Alex continued. 'Is that okay?'

'That's absolutely fine. I'm usually there till five-thirty anyway, but I'll make sure to hang on till you arrive, so don't worry if you get held up,' Simon replied, imagining the relief he would feel when Flint's ashes were taken off his hands. The thought was tinged with that all-too-familiar worry that Alex would remain good to her word and collect them as agreed.

Like every other funeral director in the land, Simon had a constant stock of ashes languishing on his shelves; some genuinely just waiting to be collected, but others forgotten and unlikely ever to be claimed. He couldn't afford for Flint's to be among them.

'We'll be there well before then,' Alex replied, as if having read Simon's thoughts.

The door swung open again behind them and Darren and Brian emerged with the floral MUM.

'Just keep it here a second,' Simon instructed, anxious to keep everyone corralled in the seclusion of the walkway and under the watchful eye of the police officer.

'Have they been here all along?' Tara asked, pointing across at the officer.

Simon was surprised she hadn't seen them when she'd first arrived. Although they'd been in an unmarked car it must surely have been obvious who they were. And he'd already told Alex that there would be a couple of police officers there anyway.

But if Tara hadn't noticed the police, did that mean that she, Alex or Carl hadn't seen that Carl's friends were there either? It was difficult to imagine how. Although if they'd arrived early and been shown straight into the chapel, then perhaps Carl's friends had arrived behind them.

Or maybe Carl did know that they'd been there and that was why he was keeping his distance now.

Simon imagined encountering Carl's car pulled up at the roadside on the way back, the traffic all snarled up around it as other drivers stopped to watch him having a blazing row with Alex and Tara if they did find out that his friends had been spectating.

But before Simon had a chance to respond to Tara's remark he heard Diane's voice say calmly but firmly: 'They were just y'ere to make sure you 'ad some peace and privacy.'

Simon and Tara both turned round to find Diane standing by the chapel door.

Simon tensed, hoping Diane wouldn't say anything about Carl's friends; but Tara was already turning her attention to the MUM cradled in Darren's arms. 'I'm going to put that on Mum's grave,' she said.

'Yes, that would be nice,' Alex replied, sounding almost motherly herself. 'Shall we do that on the way back?'

'Carl and me can do it later.'

'We can do it together on the way back,' Alex persisted.

'Darren will take it round to your car for you then,' Simon offered, by way of defusing the moment.

'Thank you,' Alex replied. And then fixing Simon with her ice-blue eyes, she added: 'And thank you for everything that you've done for us. I know you've had to take some risks because of us.'

'Yeah, thank you,' Tara added. 'It was much nicer than I thought we'd be allowed to have. And you made Dad look really nice too, the other night.'

Tara hesitated, then to Simon's surprise she stepped forward and gave him a hug.

Feeling undone, Simon defaulted to a tight-lipped smile. 'I just hope we –' he gestured to Philip and Diane, 'managed to make it what you wanted it to be.'

'It was,' Tara responded.

Simon wondered if, behind their very different facades, Alex and Tara were really just two very vulnerable young women who even now didn't really know what sort of treatment they should expect to receive from the world as the daughters of a serial murderer.

Alex turned her attention to Diane and Philip. 'Thank you for letting us come here and for conducting such a nice ceremony. We really do appreciate everything you've done for us.' And to Simon's utter amazement Tara then gave them a hug each too.

'Everyone has the right to a proper funeral, and I'm just sorry you've 'ad to come all this way to 'ave it,' Diane said, visibly moved. 'But maybe it was for the best this way.'

'I think it was actually,' Alex replied, prompting Simon to feel another swell of gratitude and admiration towards Diane.

He remained there with her and Philip as they watched Alex and Tara walk away with Darren in tow, still cradling the MUM in his outstretched forearms.

Carl dropped the butt of his second cigarette onto the paving, crushed it beneath his boot and scuffed it into the flower bed, like he'd done with the first. He walked on ahead of Alex and Tara, shooting a hostile glance at the police officer as he rounded the corner back towards the car park.

'That was a thoughtful move that, 'aving those flowers,' Diane said.

'I had a bit of a lightbulb moment when I first met with Alex and Tara and they talked about losing their mother before the murders started,' Simon replied. 'And much as I loathe letter frames, I knew one would have its uses today.'

'It certainly did. Just as well you warned me you were going to be bringing it, mind,' Diane responded. 'I was already on tenter'ooks about this funeral as it was and I'd 'ave 'ad a right panic if I'd seen you turning up with a big floral MUM!

'But it was lovely how you both made their mother part of the funeral. It's so sad, isn't it? To think of those two girls 'aving to cope with everything they've 'ad to. Anyway, I'm glad it's over with. The coffin's gone through to the cremator now.'

'Thank you for letting us come here Diane,' Philip said. 'I'm afraid you've got me to blame for recommending you to Simon when he was struggling to find somewhere.'

'Aye, so I y'eard ... I won't lie – there were times when I wondered if I'd done the right thing by agreeing to have it y'ere. But you've 'ad to risk more than I 'ave. Don't get me wrong Simon, I'm not criticising you for doing the funeral, but you know what I mean.'

'I know exactly what you mean; and you're absolutely right,' Simon said with a wan smile.

'Still, it's done now,' Diane declared. 'And you'll be back to collect the ashes tomorrow morning?'

'Ten o'clock, as agreed. I won't leave those ashes here for a moment longer than they need to be.

'Thank you.' Then turning to Philip, Diane added: 'D'you need anything from the vestry?'

'No, I made a point of travelling light for this one,' Philip replied, holding up his presentation folder.

He never rushed away after funerals anyway, and although but he would have been well within his rights to have exited stage left the moment he'd completed this one, Simon was all the more grateful that he hadn't. It felt like an act of solidarity.

'Right you are. I'll say goodbye then,' Diane said. 'I want to have a quick word with that police officer before he disappears.' She headed off down the walkway.

'I'd like to have a quick word with him myself in just a second,' Simon called after her. 'Just to find out if that couple *did* manage to get any photos of us in the end.'

Diane turned round. 'They didn't get the chance. I can tell you that for a fact. The other officer took their phones off them before you arrived and told them they wouldn't get them back until the funeral had started and they'd agreed to vacate the premises. So you 'aven't got anything to worry about on that score.'

'Oh, that's great! Thank you Diane!' Simon gushed, feeling an immense weight lifting from his shoulders. Then to Philip he said: 'D'you think we'll regret doing this funeral?'

'I think we'll find out pretty quickly if we do,' came the reply. 'But we've done nothing wrong. Alex and Tara wanted to have a funeral for their father and that's what we've given them. So come on, let's get away from here.'

Simon held out his hand. 'Thank you so much for doing this, Philip. I mean it.'

'I don't regret it, Simon; I honestly don't,' Philip responded as they shook hands. 'But if we do find ourselves on the Ten O'Clock News then make sure you chuck your hat through the door before you call me for the next one!'

'As long as you don't put your fees up too,' Simon grinned.

He went across to re-join the bearers with a deep sense of pride at what had been achieved that afternoon, and a genuine sense of privilege at having been there to witness it.

Inevitably there was much that Philip hadn't been able to touch on: so many things that had to remain unsaid. But it had still been one of the most sincere and authentic funerals that Simon had ever witnessed. And even the floral MUM had its place in the proceedings. It had never just been about camouflage.

But he was the one in need of camouflage now. His reputation – and that of the firm – would now rest solely on the hope that only the barest facts of Flint's funeral would ever become publicly known.

For all of Diane's generous cooperation and Philip's professionalism and solidarity, they were the only two people who would ever truly understand what it was that he'd done for Alex and Tara – and why.

Quite what the victims' families would make of it all when they found out, heaven only knew. They were the only people with a genuine right to an opinion on the matter, although in truth even they weren't the people whose reactions Simon was most concerned about right then.

As well as the residents of Bybrook and surrounding areas – all of whom were potential future clients– his most immediate worry was the reaction from the bereaved families he was currently working with. If he were to be exposed as the funeral director responsible for Jonathan Flint's funeral, would he be able to find a way of glossing over the fact that Flint had temporarily lain amongst their loved ones?

TWELVE

'So they definitely managed to stop those wretches getting any photos of us then?' Simon said, settling himself in the hearse.

'Yes, they did,' David confirmed. 'The officer I was talking to said that he and his colleague confiscated their phones on the spot and told them they wouldn't get them back until they agreed to leave again. But apparently they were only after a photo of the coffin, so once we'd carried it in they agreed to sling their hooks anyway.'

'They'd managed to get a couple of shots of the crematorium itself,' David continued, 'but the officers checked they'd deleted them as well, so I really don't think you've got anything at all to worry about.'

'It all went off okay though, didn't it?'

Simon had to smile to himself. Only an ex-policeman would say that about a serial killer's funeral. 'Yes, it went very well.

'Anyway, home David and don't spare the horses,' Simon added with faux weariness as he reached for his seatbelt. He was still feeling peculiarly sedated and he would have liked to linger there awhile just to enjoy the feeling while it still lasted.

He would also have liked a few moments to reflect on what he'd actually been responsible for making happen that afternoon. But he knew that any sense of achievement would only become valid once he'd safely put a decent number of miles between himself and the crematorium.

As the hearse pulled away, Simon's thoughts strayed back to the very earliest days of his career and to the memory of a conversation he'd had with his former employer's father.

Old Mr Blake, as he'd been referred to in the firm, had been the second-generation proprietor of Thomas Blake & Son in Sherwell, and Simon had been fascinated to hear the tale of how he'd conducted the funeral of a German pilot whose aircraft had crashed near the town during the war.

During the summer of 1940, a Junkers bomber on its way to attack a well-known aircraft factory near Gloucester had been brought down a few miles outside of Sherwell by a Hurricane from a local RAF airfield. Three of the German crew had successfully bailed out of their stricken aircraft, parachuting straight into the hands of stunned locals. But the pilot's parachute had failed to open and his body had later been found hanging in a tree. He was buried with full military honours in Sherwell Cemetery a week later.

Old Mr Blake had told the story without the least trace of rancour toward the German airman and he'd clearly felt no moral qualms about laying the fallen enemy to rest. Indeed, he'd seemed rather proud of it, given that a large number of local people had apparently turned out to pay their respects.

Simon recalled being rather touched at the idea of the locals all rallying round to ensure a dignified burial for the unfortunate pilot, but they'd doubtless done so in the hope that the Germans would be affording the same honour to their husbands and sons.

There weren't any parallels between the German airman and Jonathan Flint, of course. For one thing, only one of them was technically guilty of deliberate mass murder. But wasn't what they'd just done for Flint still similar in its way to what

Old Mr Blake and a cast of locals had done for the airman all those years ago?

'We do pray for mercy, and that same prayer doth teach us all to render the deeds of mercy,' as Shakespeare had put it.

But holding a funeral for someone whose crimes were as serious as Flint's really was something of a post-modern phenomenon. Right up until the final years of capital punishment in the 1960s, convicted murderers had been consigned to an unmarked grave behind prison walls:

'You be taken from this place to a lawful prison and thence to a place of execution, and that you there suffer death by hanging; and that your body be afterwards buried within the precincts of the prison in which you shall have been confined before your execution ...'

Maybe the powers-that-be had just been worried about executed criminals becoming figures of martyrdom. But maybe it was a perpetuation of the age-old notion that because the crime of murder was beyond the pale, so should its perpetrators continue to be kept away from society even in death.

But the abolition of the death penalty in 1965 had meant that responsibility for disposing of dead criminals would in future pass into the hands of professionals like Simon; for not only had hanging been consigned to the history books, but so too the ability of the state to consign its most notorious dead to an unmarked prison grave.

Cremation became the only acceptable alternative. But not only did the average crematorium lack the anonymity and security of a prison burial ground; by its very nature it also risked creating a perception in the public's mind that even the country's most reviled criminals would still receive an undeservedly dignified send-off. And even more unpalatable was the prospect of loved ones potentially having to pass through the same facilities as convicted murderers.

But how much more unpalatable would it be for people to learn that in Jonathan Flint's case, not only had one of the country's most prolific serial killers been taken to a public crematorium, but also given a funeral ceremony in its chapel?

It was 6.15 pm when David steered the hearse back into the yard and although nothing had yet appeared on the news – either on the radio or on his smartphone – Simon still couldn't help nursing irrational thoughts that the firm's involvement in Flint's funeral might already have been revealed while they'd been out, and that even then someone might be lying in wait further up the footpath, watching and waiting for the guilty wanderers to return.

Simon offered to put the hearse away and as the others made a beeline for the toilet or went to gather up belongings and car keys, he reversed the 19ft foot Mercedes back into the garage, mercifully unscathed from its mission. It was probably the longest journey the hearse had ever made and Simon felt another wave of satisfaction as he locked it away for the night, knowing that as the engine heat dissipated, so the immediate physical traces of the firm's involvement with Flint's funeral would fade with it.

Grateful for the solitude as he got upstairs to the office, he cast an anxious glance at his desk, fully expecting to see Post-It notes from Beverley warning him that she'd had journalists on the phone, along with angry relatives demanding to know if their loved ones had been stored alongside Jonathan Flint. But to his great relief his desk was as empty as he'd left it.

He knew he should quit while he was ahead and make a clean break for home, but he couldn't resist switching his computer back on before he left.

A quick trawl of the national newspaper websites revealed no mention of the funeral, but his heart missed a beat when he opened the Gloucestershire Standard website and was immediately confronted with the headline: 'Jonathan Flint: victim's mother says killer's body should be "treated with respect".' His insides once more twisting with apprehension, Simon clicked on the link.

'The mother of one of the seven young girls killed by Jonathan Flint has called for the multiple murderer to be laid to rest "with dignity".

'Karen Heaton's thirteen-year-old daughter Lucy was abducted by Flint in Cheltenham in October 2007 and he is also still regarded as the prime suspect in the unsolved disappearance of fifteen year-old Emma Simms from Westoncote in January 2007.

Emma Simms attended the same school as Flint's two daughters and it is for the sake of those daughters that Mrs Heaton, speaking on BBC Radio Cotswolds' Talkback programme, has called for Flint to be given a 'dignified' funeral.

'Her call comes after Severnside City Council and West Cotswold Borough Council issued a joint statement saying that they will refuse to accept Flint's body at any of their crematoria or cemeteries. Local residents had already been gathering outside the gates of Tredworth Crematorium in Gloucester and Churston Park Crematorium in Cheltenham, angered by the possibility of Flint's funeral taking place at either facility following his death on 7 March.

'A Severnside city councillor, quoted anonymously on the Talkback programme, said that: "Neither Sherwell District Council, Severnside City or West Cotswolds Borough Councils have any control over Mr Flint's funeral arrangements and we will simply have to wait and see what they will consist of.

'"But we sincerely hope that they will not in any way cause further distress to the victims' families or to the wider community and that the funeral will be held discreetly and preferably somewhere outside of Gloucestershire."

'However, Karen Heaton still wants Flint to be treated with dignity: "Everyone needs to be treated with respect in death and Flint's daughters should be allowed to lay their father to rest in a way that enables them to grieve properly.

'"I have heard about the protesters outside the crematorium gates and I can't bear the thought of people hurling abuse at that man's hearse or trying to disrupt his funeral. To use his dead body as a focus for anger and revenge is disgusting and inhuman, and all this talk of refusing him a proper cremation or burial is stupid and repulsive.

'"That man is dead and I firmly believe that there's a higher court that he will now have to stand before, so let his daughters lay his body to rest with dignity and privacy. They are innocent members of his family and having already lost him to the evil that led him to commit his crimes, they should at least be allowed to mourn him as the father they knew."

'Mrs Heaton – a devout Christian – has spoken before about how her faith has influenced her attitude towards her daughter's killer, a man who died without showing any remorse for his horrific crimes.

'"As Christians we are taught that forgiveness is the only way that we can move forward with our lives. I can't forgive Jonathan Flint for what he did to my daughter, or to the other girls and young women whose lives he took. And it's not my right to forgive him on their behalf anyway. But I can't stay silent about anything which encourages rage and hatred and revenge-seeking towards him, especially now that he's dead.

'"If I give in to hatred and revenge it will only trap me in the same pain that I felt when Lucy died. It would also prevent me from making the best of my life without her and I will not allow Flint to destroy my life like he destroyed Lucy's and those of the other girls.

"'How can I possibly do anything worthwhile with the rest of my life if I allow myself to become trapped in a vicious circle of rage and hatred? It would dishonour Lucy's memory and I want her to be remembered for who she was in life, not for how she died. I don't want my memories of Lucy to be tainted by hatred towards the man who took her from me."

'Although Mrs Heaton has said she would prefer it if Flint's funeral was not held in Gloucestershire, spokespeople for both the Prison Service and the West Mercia Coroner's Office have said that no further update is available on whether funeral arrangements have been made.'

With his elbows still planted on his desk, Simon pressed his palms together in front of his face and for the second time that day his eyes moistened with tears.

When he'd agreed to take the funeral on, he'd known that the only reward he could ever hope to receive would be the satisfaction of knowing that it had been carried out safely, discreetly and anonymously.

Only time would tell if he'd been able to achieve that third and final aim. But in the meantime, just being there to witness Tara's last, faltering farewell to her father was validation enough for all that he'd put himself through.

But never for one moment had he imagined that absolution, affirmation even, would come from one of the victims' mothers – and none other than Marie Sandbrook's friend at that. And it was just so reassuring to know that, in Karen Heaton's view at least, it seemed that he really had done the right thing after all.

THIRTEEN

Simon arrived back at Llancroes at 9.40 am. Mourners were gathering for the 10 o'clock and he couldn't help but feel a certain thrill at returning to the scene of the crime.

He'd monitored the news constantly from when he'd got home after the funeral right through to 1.00 am, when he'd finally gone to bed. And the first thing he'd done on waking up again at 6.30 was check his smartphone. But still there was no mention of the funeral and, feeling as if a huge shadow was finally lifting from him, he was daring himself to believe that he really had succeeded in sneaking the whole thing under the radar.

But ever since switching off his computer and locking up the office the evening before, he'd been haunted by Karen Heaton's unwitting plea for Flint to be afforded some dignity in death.

Only a mother could have wished for such consideration for Alex and Tara, and Karen Heaton's words had prompted him into a night spent in sober reflection on the sanctimonious pride with which he'd approached the task of arranging the funeral.

The two administrators looked up from their work with expectant expressions when Simon stepped up to the reception counter.

'Ah, we were waiting for you. You'd better come round,' Jean said, getting up from her desk and opening the door next to the reception window. 'Have you been getting phone calls from the newspapers too?'

Simon felt himself blanch, but before he had a chance to ask Jean what she meant, Diane appeared.

'Simon! Thank you for coming back so quick. I'll be a lot happier when these ashes are gone now. I've already had the Daily Mirror and the Daily Express on this morning.'

Like a dying man seeing images from his life flashing in front of him, thoughts of the previous day's events and the lengths he'd gone to in making them happen, all tumbled through Simon's mind. News of the funeral was always going to break at some point, but he couldn't help but feel embarrassed and even a little incompetent to be finding out like this.

'I've been checking the internet news constantly since the moment we left here yesterday and I haven't seen a thing. What did they say when they phoned?'

'They'd y'eard that the funeral 'ad taken place at a crematorium in South Wales and they were phoning to see if it was y'ere. There wasn't much point in denying it.'

'No ... no, of course not.'

'They also knew that it was his daughters and a partner who'd attended and they wanted to know what sort of service it was and who'd taken it. I just told them it had been a very brief, non-religious ceremony, but I didn't mention anything about Mr Coleridge or you.'

'Thank you,' Simon said contritely. 'It must have been that wretched couple that turned up yesterday who blew the whistle.'

'Course it was!' Diane responded. 'But just be thankful they didn't manage to get any photos too.'

'Yes, that's true ...' Simon murmured. 'Did the newspapers know anything about the music?'

'No. All they seemed to know, apart from it being at a crem' in South Wales and about the two daughters attendin', was that other crematoria had already turned it away. I said I couldn't make any comment about that and I said to them what I said to you: that I'd agreed to have the funeral y'ere purely on y'umanitarian grounds.'

Feeling chastised again, Simon tried to marshal his thoughts. Embarrassing though it was to discover that Diane had already been firefighting for him, things were actually still going to plan; provided the media didn't try digging any further. If they did, they'd be sure to find their way to his door eventually.

'I'm very sorry you've had to put up with that this morning, Diane. Maybe I was being too naïve in thinking we might get away with it. But after the all lengths we went to, and then for it to be that idiot Carl of all people to blow our cover ... Well, I despair ... I really do.'

'It's not your fault. Don't go beatin' yourself up about it. We both knew the press would get hold of it sooner or later. The important thing is we managed to get the funeral done before they *did* find out. Anyway, it doesn't really affect anything y'ere. As long as you take those ashes off my 'ands now, then I can cope with a few more phone calls if I 'ave to.

'Next thing is the local rag will be all over it like a rash, but I'm used to dealing with them. It'll be the biggest story they've 'ad in a while, mind!'

Simon didn't want to admit it, but that particular thought had already occurred to him; and in between checking the news the previous evening, he'd dug out another book from the varied contents of his shelves, about the infamous occultist Aleister Crowley.

Remembering that there had been a great deal of controversy surrounding Crowley's funeral at Brighton

Crematorium in 1947, he'd decided to look up the details, just in case there was anything to be learnt from it.

Crowley, who'd referred to himself as the 'Great Beast' and who was referred to by others as the 'wickedest man alive', was widely regarded as a Satanist. His reputation was such that his funeral ceremony had caused a huge outcry amongst the people of Brighton and Hove, who'd been left terrified by wildly exaggerated claims in the newspapers of a black mass having been held in their local crematorium. The reality had been rather more prosaic, even if by the standards of the time the ceremony probably had still bordered on the outright blasphemous.

It had actually just consisted of readings from Crowley's own works. Crematorium time slots were often limited to twenty minutes in those days, so there wouldn't have been time for anything very elaborate anyway. Certainly not enough time for a black mass.

But the local council had declared the funeral a desecration of a consecrated space and a prayer meeting had been hastily organised in the town's main church in an effort to counteract the malevolent forces feared to have been released during Crowley's funeral.

Simon wondered whether Flint's funeral would elicit similar feelings amongst the townsfolk of Llancroes. Would they feel a similar sense of outrage and desecration on hearing that their local crematorium had hosted the funeral of a reviled serial rapist and murderer? And an English one at that . . . ?

'Anyway, I'll get the ashes and in the nicest possible way get you off the premises again.' Diane said with a sly smile. She went back out the door at the rear of the office and reappeared clutching a burgundy 'polytainer' – a plastic urn shaped like a sweet jar, with a screw-on lid oddly similar to the ones on coffee jars.

'I've kept the certificate to one side, Di,' Jean said, reaching into a wire tray on her desk. She handed the envelope across.

Diane compared the cremation number on the envelope with the stick-on label on the polytainer. 'Whereabouts are you parked?' She said as she opened the ashes collection register and pointed to where Simon had to sign.

'Over in the main car park,' he replied. 'But I've come prepared.' From his jacket pocket he extracted a Lewiston-issue burgundy carrier bag printed with a gold rose design.

'Good thinking! But we always get our funeral directors to park outside y'ere when they're collecting ashes.' Diane gestured towards the window. 'Mainly because none of them have the sense that you've 'ad to bring something to put them in. But even so, I don't like 'aving funeral staff wanderin' round the grounds with polytainers or caskets stuck under their arms.'

'I understand. I'll go and bring my car round,' Simon said politely.

He strode back round to the car park, shooting a guilty glance at the newly-arrived ten o'clock as he did so. It was the first funeral since Flint's and the scene could hardly have been more different.

The immediate family – a wife and daughters by the looks of it – were stood in a tearful huddle, staring at the coffin in the back of the hearse. The rest of the mourners were gathered at the end of the footpath from the car park; and strutting about in the midst of it all was a very self-important-looking young funeral director with top hat in one hand and silver-topped cane in the other.

There was nothing wrong with the hat, but Simon thought the cane was a pointless affectation. Quite apart from making the funeral director look like Bertie Wooster, he could have done with having his hands free for more important things.

But the sight of him reminded Simon of how, as a twenty year-old novice, he'd been bursting with pride when he'd put on his new top hat and walked in front of the hearse for the first time. The thought of it made his insides curdle now.

He'd grown weary of the pomp and ceremony that his role required on funerals and he detested being on show nowadays. But families did still like having the funeral director lead the cortege on foot; and for all that they increasingly claimed to dislike the black-clad formality of funerals, they loved it when the traffic was halted for a few moments and their loved one's passing was made to feel just that little bit more important in the midst of a busy world.

But that wasn't an excuse for over-enthusiastic funeral directors to be strutting their stuff on the public highway or using the crematorium driveway as a catwalk. Yes, they were there to put on a bit of a show, but it was the deceased who was supposed to have the starring role.

There were a few too many funeral directors out there who failed to appreciate that it wasn't simply a profession, but a daily negotiation between the profound and the prosaic. A dance between the sacred, the secular and sometimes the downright surreal. And that to be truly effective within their role, they needed to be honest with themselves about what their real motivations were for doing it.

If it was simply a desire for status in their community, then they were in the wrong job. But if it was the prospect of being able to draw alongside the newly-bereaved and act as their guide and support that fired their imagination, they still needed to be sure that their intentions were entirely baggage-free, because it simply wasn't feasible to approach funeral work pre-loaded. The bereaved were endangered enough already.

Simon was only too aware that he had recklessly endangered himself now. That despite his years of experience he'd been naïve enough to think that it would be possible to handle a funeral like Flint's and still have it within his power to avoid the consequences. And watching that young funeral director very diligently going about his duties right then, Simon couldn't help but feel just a little bit jealous.

He got back into his car and drove round to the office. He checked that the Certificate for Disposal of Cremated Remains was tucked inside the carrier bag alongside the ashes and then bade a grateful and somewhat sheepish farewell to Diane Roberts, the woman without whose generous cooperation the remains of Jonathan Flint, serial killer, wouldn't now be reduced to the consistency of coarse sand, and the volumetric equivalent of three bags of sugar.

Despite the countless sets of ashes he'd handled over the years, Simon couldn't help but think it rather surreal that the cause of so much horror and notoriety should now amount to nothing more than the dusty contents of a plastic jar. And given the sterile, granular state that Flint was now in, Simon thought it was all the more unjust that he might yet have to answer for his part in turning the serial murderer to dust.

Casting another glance at the carrier bag sat on his passenger seat when he got back onto the motorway, he reflected on the three very different trips he'd made up and down the M5 with Flint on board. Then following an Abba song the radio DJ introduced the news. The urgent-sounding jingle that followed was accompanied by the newsreader listing the headlines, of which the second one was that: 'A funeral service for convicted serial murderer Jonathan Flint has taken place.'

Simon's stomach lurched and he suddenly felt light-headed.

The sensation panicked him sufficiently enough that for a few seconds he wondered if he should pull onto the hard shoulder. But the very last thing he wanted to do now was to risk stranding himself at the side of the motorway with Flint's ashes in the car, so he took a deep breath and forced himself to calm down.

The first news item seemed to take an age for the newsreader to get through, but finally: 'A funeral service has taken place for Jonathan Flint, convicted in 2008 of raping and murdering seven young women and teenage girls. A statement issued by the Prison Service confirmed that Flint, who died in hospital on the seventh of March at the age of fifty-two, was cremated yesterday in a private, non-religious service attended only by his two daughters. The funeral took place at a crematorium in South Wales.

'Superintendent John Pearson of South Wales Police said that Mr Flint's family were still just as entitled as any other family to grieve in peace and privacy, and that a discreet police presence had been provided at the crematorium to ensure that a dignified ceremony could take place.

'The news comes just a day after Karen Heaton, whose thirteen-year-old daughter Lucy was murdered by Jonathan Flint in 2007, said in an interview on BBC Radio Cotswolds' Talkback programme that Flint should be treated with respect in death, and that for the sake of his daughters he should be laid to rest with dignity and privacy.'

As the newsreader moved onto the next item, Simon glanced across at the carrier bag again, feeling a renewed sense of responsibility towards its contents.

*

Holding the plastic funnel firmly over the top of the polytainer, Simon inverted them both and rested the funnel on the rim of the decorative scattering urn.

It would have been more appropriate just to leave Flint's ashes in the polytainer, but Simon knew from experience that scattering ashes was enough of a challenge as it was: Sod's Law dictated that there would always be *someone* around – be they dog walker, rambler, mountain biker or other assorted menace to privacy – and there was no clearer signal that you weren't just there to enjoy the scenery than having a polytainer tucked under your arm as you scouted around for a suitable spot.

Alex and Tara simply couldn't afford to be left in that position.

Having decanted the ashes into the urn, Simon couldn't resist stroking his fingertips through the coarse, grey granules. The man whose story had been told in countless newspaper, magazine and internet articles and any number of books and television programmes, and whose image had been immortalised in family photos and police mugshots released to the press, and by press photographs during his transfer to and from prison vans, was now nothing more than a couple of kilograms of pulverised bone.

His body had been subjected to 800°C heat until the soft tissues had been completely destroyed. Then the heat-shattered remains of his bones had been raked up, cooled and pulverised into thick grey granules of calcium and phosphate, without any trace of DNA left to identify them.

What more could have been done to erase the traces of evil? What more harm could Jonathan Flint cause to anyone now? His ashes were neither a threat to public health nor an affront to public decency. And yet, because they were *his* cremated remains they would still hold totemic status in the eyes of those who had suffered as a result of his crimes, as well as in the eyes of the inevitable few who would be ghoulish and twisted enough to venerate him.

So how best to dispose of them?

Denying Flint's ashes an identifiable burial place wouldn't eradicate him from history. But at least if they were scattered as widely and as anonymously as possible, then it could be claimed that Flint's physical presence had been all but eradicated. Dust amongst the dust.

*

Alex and Tara arrived at 4.50 pm. Deeply relieved that they'd stayed true to their word, Simon led them into the arranging lounge and went back upstairs to fetch the ashes.

The funeral had by then been reported by all the national newspapers and news websites. Diane Roberts' phrase 'on humanitarian grounds' had been extensively quoted, but mercifully the extent of the information published had been confined to the fact that a simple, non-religious ceremony had taken place at Llancroes Crematorium in South Wales and that it had been attended only by Flint's two daughters (Alex and Tara weren't referred to by name in any of the articles). Crucially there was no mention of the music and no photographs, other than of the crematorium itself in some of the reports.

And to his even greater relief, Simon hadn't received any phone calls or approaches from the media – with the exception of Joanne Barrett, who'd assumed that a funeral director in South Wales had handled the funeral in the end. Simon was more than happy to sponsor that assumption.

So all in all, things appeared to have worked out rather well.

Simon carried the urn downstairs, supporting its weight with one hand while holding the cord handles of its floral-printed carrying bag with the other. Then, as he did with all ashes hand-overs, he put the bag down on the coffee table before reverently lifting the urn from it and putting it back down on the table.

'The urn itself is cardboard, so it's completely disposable. The lid just lifts off,' he lifted it a few millimetres to demonstrate, 'and then you just need to undo the cotton liner inside.'

Receiving the usual nods and murmurs of understanding, he then extracted the envelope marked 'Certificate for Disposal of Cremated Remains' from the carry bag.

'When ashes are going to be buried in a churchyard or cemetery this certificate has to be handed to the church or burial authority—'

'We're not *going* to bury them in a churchyard,' Tara interjected.

To Simon's disappointment, but not remotely to his surprise, she was back to her usual prickly self.

'No, I realise that,' he responded patiently. 'And because you *are* going to be scattering the ashes privately, this certificate is redundant. But I'll leave it with the ashes anyway, just as proof of identity.'

Alex gave another murmur of understanding, but Tara wasn't satisfied: 'How do we know those really are his ashes though?'

'That's why he's just said about the certificate,' Alex responded.

'A certificate doesn't mean anything,' came the reply.

'The whole cremation process is enshrined in law,' Simon began once more. 'It's physically impossible to fit more than one coffin in a cremator anyway, but there's a strict chain of identity throughout the process, from the moment the coffin arrives at the crematorium right through to when the ashes are put into the urn afterwards. So I can assure you, there's no question whatsoever that these are your father's ashes.'

Tara had no response to that, so Simon continued: 'One thing I will say though – and I say this to every family who intend to scatter ashes – is that there's more in the urn than you might think. It's not like you see on the telly where someone just sprinkles a handful of dust.'

Alex pressed both her hands round the urn and gently hefted it off the table. 'Gosh, I see what you mean …'

Tara looked genuinely shocked by her sister's casual handling of the urn.

'It's about the same quantity as three bags of sugar. So depending on where you have in mind to scatter the ashes, the wider you can spread them, the less visible they'll be and the more quickly they'll be absorbed into the ground.'

'I understand,' Alex replied.

'So …' Simon said with a suitably reluctant sigh, 'unless there's anything else you think I can help you with, this is where my involvement comes to an end. How and where you choose to lay your father to rest is entirely a matter for the two of you to decide from here.'

'Thank you for everything you've done,' Alex said as Simon gently lowered the urn back into the carrying bag. 'You made the funeral so much nicer than we ever thought it would be. And you've been really kind to us all the way through it all. We do appreciate it.'

'Well, like I said at the beginning, as far as I'm concerned, he is still your father,' Simon said with a sorrowful smile.

Having walked this final part of their eleven-year journey with them, he hoped that Alex and Tara would remember him as someone a little more than just the last in a long line of professionals they'd found themselves having to deal with over that time.

FOURTEEN

Simon led the bearers out of the chapel and pulled the heavy, oak door closed behind them. He retrieved a set of cremation forms from the hearse, handed them to Brian and asked him to drop them round to the office and collect a set of ashes while he was there. He told Darren where he wanted the hearse moved to and where the flowers needed to be put out on display and then turned to where Patrick was rolling one of his customary cigarettes in the corner of the archway by the vestry door.

'You busy?' Patrick said.

'Just ticking along. What's it like with everyone else?'

'The Co-Op 'ave got a bit of a rush on, but they're the only ones what 'ave.'

'Oh, right.'

'Eh, you 'an't 'eard this from me, but one of Jonathan Flint's daughters killed theirselves last night.'

Simon felt his stomach lurch, and as he deployed his best poker face, his body temperature felt like it had plummeted.

'Thurlow and Ball were up 'ere earlier an' two of their blokes did a coroner's removal last night,' Patrick continued. 'Woman in her twenties found dead from an overdose. T and B were given a name when they took the call, but the daughters 'ad their names changed after their father was locked up, didn't 'um?'

'Yeah . . . they did,' Simon agreed, his heart thumping.

'Anyway, when the blokes got there they said it were more like a murder scene – all cordoned off an' loads of police. They asked what was going on an' one of the police officers told 'em it was actually one of Flint's daughters.

'Fuckin' sad mind. But after everything that 'appened with her father, maybe she just couldn't take it all no more.'

'Where was the removal?' Simon asked, swallowing down a genuine swell of emotion. Thurlow and Ball were a Cheltenham firm.

'Some new-build estate out by Cheltenham Racecourse.'

The confirmation still came like a body blow, and with it a powerful sense of helplessness.

Given the years that Alex and Tara had spent exiled in anonymity, Simon knew he was amongst the few people to have engaged with them on the basis of their true identities; and he was filled with a sudden and very proprietorial desire for it to be known that he was the funeral director who had handled Jonathan Flint's funeral, and that he might therefore have some unique insights to offer towards the investigation into Alex's death.

'I take it T and B were just called off the rota, were they?' he asked. 'You don't think it was them that did Jonathan Flint's funeral, do you?'

'No, it weren't them. It were prob'ly just their turn on the police rota. Anyway, old Jonny Flint ended up goin' to South Wales didn't 'e? So whichever firm did 'is funeral down there will prob'ly end up doin' the daughter's as well now.'

I hope so, Simon thought to himself.

*

The police issued a short statement the following day, explaining that Alexandra Turner – a twenty-six year-old laboratory supervisor found dead in her flat in Prestbury Heights, Cheltenham, was in fact Alexandra Flint – eldest daughter of deceased serial murderer Jonathan Flint. The statement went on to say that her death was not being treated as suspicious and that a file was being prepared for the coroner. Police-speak for suicide, in other words.

Over the next twenty-four hours Simon monitored the internet constantly, and although the story inevitably received greater coverage on the websites of tabloid newspapers rather than their broadsheet counterparts, none of them revealed anything that Simon didn't already know. Not until the story exploded onto all the front pages three days later:

'A search team from Gloucestershire Police have begun combing an area of woodland at Brockham, between Gloucester and Westoncote, the village from where fifteen-year-old Emma Simms disappeared without trace in 2007.

'It has long been suspected that Simms could have been the first victim of Gloucestershire serial killer Jonathan Flint, who died in March this year, ten years into a life sentence for the rape and murder of seven young women and girls. And in what can only be regarded as a significant development, the search work comes just three days after Flint's eldest daughter Alexandra – who'd been living under a new identity since her father's conviction in 2008 – was found dead in her Cheltenham home.

'Emma Simms was a pupil at the same school as Alexandra and her sister Tara. On the night she disappeared, Emma had called round to a house in her home village of Westoncote where she knew Alexandra was babysitting. Emma had then gone back to Alexandra's house, from where she left an hour later to walk back to her own home. But despite Alexandra later receiving a text message from Emma to say that she'd got home safely, Emma was never seen again.

'When police interviewed Alexandra following her father's arrest for the seven murders for which he was later convicted, she was able to state that her father had been at home with her, her sister Tara and their terminally ill mother throughout the night that her school friend disappeared.

'Detective Chief Inspector Jeremy Carter, in charge of the search, said: "This is an intelligence-led operation and forms part of an ongoing investigation," and although DCI Carter refused to say whether the search was linked to the disappearance of Emma Simms, he did confirm that the search team were "focusing their efforts on a very specific area."'

*

'I phoned the coroner's office. Alexandra Turner's cleared now and the cremation certificate will be at the mortuary,' Beverley said, glancing down at her notepad. 'And I've also had a Sergeant Simon Benson from Gloucestershire Police on the phone. Because the funeral's going to be held at Llancroes again, he wants to know if he needs to inform South Wales Police like they did last time.'

'Yeah, Colin told me I'd be getting a call from him,' Simon replied.

'I said you wouldn't be back till after twelve, so Sergeant Benson's given me his direct line and the times when he's back on shift. Anyway, how did you get on?'

Simon took out his arranging folder and stowed his briefcase back under his desk. He sat down and swivelled his chair to face Beverley.

'You mustn't breathe a word of this to anyone; but it was Colin Armstrong who first raised the alarm the day Alex was found dead.'

'It wasn't him that found her, was it?!'

'No, it's a bit more sinister than that. Colin had a special delivery letter from Alex in amongst his post the day she was found dead, asking him to handle her affairs.'

'She'd filled out one of those write-your-own-will forms and then attached a list of all her personal information: her bank details; copies of her utility bills; all her internet and computer passwords; rental details for her flat; car insurance and vehicle registration documents; literally everything you could think of.

'Then she finished her letter by saying that by the time Colin read it she would be dead and that her body could be found in her flat. And then sellotaped to the bottom was a memory stick.

'Colin phoned the police, then looked to see what was on the memory stick and found another letter from Alex, giving an account of what actually happened the night that Emma Simms disappeared.'

'Oh God ...' Beverley murmured. 'What did it say?'

'The police have sworn Colin to secrecy because of their investigation, but he thought I should know, because I'll be handling the funeral. So like I said, this absolutely cannot go any further than you and me.

'The first part of Alex's account just confirmed what's always been known: that the night Emma Simms disappeared she'd called round to a house where Alex was babysitting; and that when the child's parents came home earlier than expected, Emma had gone back to Alex's house with her.

'Emma left for her own home an hour later, and as promised she sent Alex a text message to say she'd got home safely.

'But Alex then said that her friendship with Emma had always been a bit one-sided and that Emma had always regarded them as being closer than Alex had. Alex said that she'd always thought of Emma as being a bit needy and she'd also known that Emma had a bit of a crush on her father... I know, talk about ironic,' Simon added, as Beverley give an involuntary shudder. 'But it was always said that he was a hit with the women, wasn't it? So you can just imagine an impressionable teenage girl going weak at the knees for him.'

'Don't! It makes my skin crawl just thinking about it,' Beverley responded.

'You're not the only one,' Simon said. 'Anyway, Emma had been having problems at home apparently, and she'd called round to where Alex was babysitting so they could talk in private. When they ended up back at Alex's house, Jonathan was there, because of course by that time his wife was bedridden with cancer.

'Tara had been in her bedroom all that evening and didn't even know that Emma had been there; and when Emma got ready to go home, Jonathan offered to give her a lift because he needed to nip out and collect something from his office.

'Alex said she'd expected Emma to jump at the chance, but that Emma had actually got a bit flustered and embarrassed and decided to walk home instead. But Alex then said that there was something she'd never told the police when they interviewed her after her father's arrest: that just after Emma left to go home, Jonathan had told Alex to take a drink upstairs to her mother and to sit with her for him while he nipped back to his office to get whatever it was he wanted. And that he didn't then return home until *much* later that night...'

Beverley's eyes widened and her lips parted as if to speak, but she said nothing.

'Alex wrote that Tara was never aware of events that night because she'd been in her bedroom listening to music the whole time. But that for her own part, Alex had been too frightened to say anything to the police, and that it had been eating away at her for all these years since. And that now her father's dead – and although it was purely a guess on her part, she felt she owed it to the police and to Emma Simms' family to say that there was a particular area up in Brockham Woods where her parents used to take her and Tara for walks when they were kids.'

Beverley was silent for a moment and Simon could see that she was thinking the very same thoughts that he had when he'd first heard all this for himself.

'So what are the funeral arrangements going to be then?' Beverley asked.

'Alex left instructions in this will that she drew up for herself. She wanted me to do it if possible, because I'd been so kind and professional when I did her father's funeral; she wanted to be cremated at Llancroes and she just wanted to have one particular piece of music played: a Duran Duran song that had been a favourite of her mother's.

'Then after the cremation, she wanted her ashes interred in her mother's plot at Westoncote Cemetery: but not to have her name added to the memorial stone.'

Beverley had the glasses with the purple and grey frames on that day and behind them her eyes seemed to be glistening with tears. 'So how do you feel about her now? D'you still feel sorry for her?'

'Yes, I do,' Simon replied. 'I'm not excusing her keeping quiet for all these years – but . . . I can kind of understand it.'

'But what led her to kill herself though?' Beverley asked. 'D'you think it was it just the guilt of not having said anything for all this time? Or d'you think she's always known more than she's admitted to, even now?'

'I don't know. She might have known more than she's admitted, I suppose. Or maybe she has told the full truth now and taking her own life was then simply an act of atonement.

Either that or she was just terrified of what the consequences would be of breaking her silence.'

'And what about the consequences for you now?' Beverley said. 'After everything you did to keep it quiet last time this could undo everything.'

*

Simon had sent Darren to the coroner's mortuary in the end. Although the staff there were completely neutral and probably wouldn't have said anything anyway, it was still easier just to send Darren.

But Simon was relieved by what he found now. Alex looked okay. Very peaceful in fact, in that starkly absent way that only the younger dead had about them.

Her eyes were closed and her mouth was open enough only to expose the edges of her teeth. Her auburn hair was scraped back from her face and lay lank and lustreless around her head; and her complexion was equally washed out. But better that than being stained from post-mortem lividity.

In fact, it was only her left ear that had discoloured to a reddish purple where her head had been left lying to one side. A head block would have prevented that, but the coroner's mortuary was too busy a place for such niceties.

There was a slight ridge across Alex's forehead where the cranial cap had slipped out of alignment beneath the scalp, but that was easily rectified. Simon took hold of her head and realigned the cap with his thumbs.

He could also see how misshapen her chin and throat had become, where her neck had been packed with absorbent tissue. But with a stranglehold grip of his hands – the dreadful irony wasn't lost on him – and some gentle remoulding, that too was soon rectified.

It would have been the easiest thing in the world to carry on and set the features then. But despite the gruesome indignities Alex's body had already been subjected to, there was a purity to her appearance that Simon didn't now want to sully.

He unzipped the rest of the bag, within which Alex's body was dressed in a disposable shroud. Hooking a finger round the neckline, Simon pulled the shroud down just far enough to expose a pair of delicately smooth shoulders and the meticulously neat, but viciously ugly line of post-mortem suturing that ran between them.

There was nothing like PM suturing to lay waste to an otherwise unblemished décolletage, and countless were the times that Simon had had to tactfully advise families against providing clothes with a low neckline for just that reason; but it was strangely reassuring to see the suturing now. Proof that it really was just Alex's empty shell lying there.

Simon pulled the shroud back up and then pinned one of the ears back with his finger. Sure enough, there was the other line of suturing across the back of the head. The mortuary technician must have been cursing Alex's long hair when he or she had sutured up the scalp.

Simon released the ear and leant his hands on the edge of the fridge tray, mentally juxtaposing the cold, damp form lying before him with the enigmatic young woman who'd greeted him at the door to her flat.

He pulled the unzipped bag back around Alex's body and went through to the workshop to fit and line a coffin for her. Once he'd lowered Alex's body into it, he set to work loosening her arms and unclenching her condensation-moistened fingers. Struck by how small and delicate they felt, he realised the last hands he'd done this to were those of Alex's father.

He straightened the ill-fitting shroud and tucked it around her body as best he could, before placing Alex's left hand down at her side. He then laid her right hand across her abdomen, a pose he liked to use for viewings. The randomness of it looked so much more natural than the more customary, but rather pious-looking, crossing of the hands.

He combed Alex's hair down either side of her face as nicely as he could and picked away the loose strands from her forehead. Then after checking the plastic wrist tag one last time he laid his hand over hers. 'I'm so very sorry that it's ended like this, Alex,' he murmured.

He zipped up the body bag and tucked it neatly inside the cremfilm-lined coffin. No taffeta for Alex; just a bed of white plastic. Then he put the lid on and screwed it down. It was an early start the next day. Diane Roberts had offered him another 4 o'clock slot, but he'd opted for a 9.30 – the usual time for committal-only's.

*

It was 7.30 am and the day was clearly going to be another warm and sunny one. But it wasn't just the early morning coolness of the garage that Simon valued right then, so much as the knowledge that once this sad little task was completed, he would still have a normal working day to return to.

He slid Alex's coffin into the back of his estate car and stowed the collapsible bier trolley alongside it. Her father should have been the one to get this sort of treatment, but there was no need for ceremony, let alone subterfuge, this time around. All Simon wanted to do was get down to Llancroes, sit and listen to the music Alex had chosen, then see her off and return home with a line firmly drawn under the whole sorry saga.

Fortunately – and with appalling irony – it was Emma Simms' funeral arrangements that were attracting all the attention. Barely three weeks after her remains had been discovered, they'd been released again by the coroner.

Detective Chief Inspector Jeremy Carter, the senior investigating officer from Gloucestershire Police, had confirmed at the opening of the inquest into Emma's death that her skeletal remains had been identified by dental records. It hadn't been possible to ascertain the cause of death, but strangulation was considered to be the most likely possibility; and with no trace of clothing being found at the scene, it meant that Emma's body had been naked when it was put there.

DCI Carter went on to say that the intelligence that led to the discovery of the body, coupled with the similarities to the seven murders known to have been committed by Jonathan Flint, meant that they were not looking for anyone else in connection with the death. Confirmation then, that Emma Simms had indeed fallen prey to Flint eleven years previously.

Simon's former employers – Thomas Blake and Son in Sherwell, were handling the arrangements and a death notice had appeared in that week's edition of the Sherwell Gazette: a few sparse lines announcing an end to eleven years of hope in vain and confirming the suspicions of all that time.

The service was going to be at Westoncote Parish Church, followed by burial at Westoncote Cemetery: a decent Christian burial for Emma's parents to rectify the eleven unimaginable years they had spent not knowing where their daughter was.

The funeral was going to be a desperately poignant affair, and while at any other time Simon would have been jealous of the high-profile role that his former employers would occupy within the proceedings, he was simply grateful that it would divert attention from Alex's altogether more humble and apologetic arrangements.

While his former employers would be basking in the muted glory of their tragic but honourable duties, his task was to skulk away to South Wales and quietly dispose of the young woman who for eleven years had been covering the tracks of her school friend's rapist and killer.

*

Between them, Simon, Darren and David wheeled Alex's coffin into the chapel and hoisted it onto the catafalque.

His heart pumping from the exertion of lifting the head end by himself, Simon cocked his head from left to right to check the coffin was straight; then, trying to keep his suddenly laboured breathing in check, he took a step back, paused, and in unison with Darren and David gave a curt bow. Leaving the other two to head back out with the bier trolley, Simon took his place in the same pew where Alex, Tara and Carl had sat together just four months previously.

'We have gathered quietly, unobtrusively and without any pretence that things are any different than they actually are. We have gathered in the knowledge that you recognise and acknowledge only too well how the consequences of one person's actions can have such profound and far-reaching effects on the lives of others: effects so serious that there can never be any prospect of healing...'

Duran Duran's 'Ordinary World' began to play. Simon had downloaded and listened to it constantly since learning of Alex's request for it to be played; but despite having looked up the lyrics online and searched them for meaning, he could only reflect on the irony of how, in spite of everything the song spoke about, Alex hadn't been able to find a similar strength of her own to carry on. And when he felt the inevitable prickle of tears he felt no shame in wiping them away this time.

It was impossible to imagine what Alex must have gone through when her father was first arrested; and how, still grieving for her mother, she must have been like a rabbit caught in headlights when police officers had gently but firmly told her that her father had been charged with the rape and murder of not just one young girl, but seven; and that she must now put aside any sense of loyalty to him and tell them everything she knew.

In circumstances like that, how could a shocked and terrified teenage girl have been expected to remember the precise details and sequence of events of a night ten months previously, when her school friend had mysteriously disappeared? Particularly when it might only serve to further seal her father's fate.

Or maybe Alex *had* remembered all too clearly and that dawning realisation had either plunged her into a state of denial, or perhaps even incited a fierce and reckless sense of loyalty toward her beleaguered father – the only parent she had left.

But whatever the truth was, what was it that had prompted her to break her silence now – and then take her own life in doing so?

> *'And neither is this the time to be looking for answers that we might never find. We are gathered here in the shadow of the unanswerable; the unthinkable; the unimaginable. But we cannot use this short time to dwell on all that has passed.'*

The song reached its final chorus and Simon stood up – the signal for Diane to remotely operate the curtains from her place at the back of the chapel. The voile began its slow traverse and the alcove lights started to dim.

> *'The innocent and the guilty stare back at us from the far reaches of time and we cannot deny their existence, however much we may want to erase them from history.'*

The velvet curtains followed, taking the coffin from sight; and it really was all over then.

Simon intended to leave it for a few weeks and let the dust settle after Emma Simms' funeral, before going up to Westoncote Cemetery and discreetly interring Alex's ashes in her mother's plot. He was still hoping that Tara might come along for that instead.

Lightning Source UK Ltd.
Milton Keynes UK
UKHW010651111120
373204UK00002B/256